DEATH IN PARADISE

DEATH IN HAWAII SERIES

J.E. TRENT

For my wife, who was a continuous source of encouragement to write this story. I'm eternally grateful.

PREQUEL OFFER

I would like to give you the e-book only prequel to this book. It tells the story of the murder of Jessica's best friend when Jessica was twenty years old.

It's only available to readers of this book. Go to the download page of *Death in Hawaii*.

1

MORNING PADDLE

Kona Hawaii

Nothing like a hot-blooded Filipino woman with a bad attitude pointing a butterfly knife at you first thing in the morning to get your adrenaline pumping. Not Mike Murphy's preferred way to start the day. Once again, Simmy had accused him of playing huggy-kissy with another woman. And he was sick of it. It was 6:30 a.m. as the sun rose over Hualalai Mountain and turned the puffy white clouds above Kailua Bay cotton candy pink.

Mike paddled his one-man canoe over the reef, heading towards Kaiwi Point. Most days he paddled south towards Keauhou. But this morning there was a fishing tournament about to start in Kona. There were twenty-five boats entered, and they were jockeying for the best position near the Kailua Pier. Mike didn't want to get tangled up with them.

Those rich bastards were trying to get the jump on the other boats at the start of the tournament. They could be cutthroat as they raced off to the fishing grounds. A canoe, versus a forty-five-foot Cabo fishing yacht, doesn't get any right-of-way. What the canoe might get was flipped by the wake. And it was too early in the morning to hui the boat as far as he was concerned.

Mike used his time on the ocean every morning to think about life and whatever he had planned for the day. Today, he had two pressing issues. A woman who loved him in an unhealthy jealous kind of way, it seemed, if he didn't do what she wanted. And a billionaire neighbor who wanted to buy his Aloha Village Resort so he could bulldoze it and add to his concrete mega-resort next door.

Mike tried to quit thinking of his crazy girlfriend and just be at one with the ocean, digging his paddle deep into the water with each stroke. His canoe was moving fast through the light swells when the first dolphin exploded out of the water. It cleared his head by mere inches as it crossed over to the starboard side and drenched him with the seawater spray flying off its body.

"Damn it, Koa!" Mike yelled at the dolphin as it swam away. He was on guard now. He knew Kiki wasn't far behind and expected her to come leaping out of the ocean any second. Hopefully not over his head, as Koa had just done. That behavior was not typical of dolphins in the wild. But these two dolphins were not wild, or normal. They were highly trained, and they belonged to Kona Jack, Mike's brother. According to the government, they belonged to the US Navy and were only in Jack's care. But, in reality, they were Jack's.

Mike reminded himself he needed to call Jack today and see if he could look into his problem neighbor. Jack Murphy had retired six months ago from NCIS in Honolulu and moved to Kona after buying a local fishing charter. Jack still had his thumb on the pulse of international crime in the Pacific region, though, and did part-time contract work for the Navy to boost his retirement income. Mike knew there was something rotten about Lau; it was a nagging feeling that wouldn't go away. But he knew Jack could figure it out.

Mr. Lau owned the Ming Resort next door to Mike's property. There was something about that guy that gave Mike a bad feeling, but he couldn't put his finger on it. Most people took no for an answer. Not Lau. The word *no* didn't seem to be in his vocabulary. Not even after Mike had told him, for the third time, that he was not interested in selling at any price. And certainly not so Lau could expand the Ming into a casino.

As Mike's canoe rounded Kaiwi Point, he decided it was time to paddle back to the pier. He needed to call Jack to see if he was back from Hong Kong yet.

After putting the canoe on top of his Tundra, he drove to the Old Kona Airport to chill at the beach while he called Jack. He parked by the first palm tree near the water, got out of the truck, and walked to the picnic table on the sand. He sat down on the bench and took a minute to check the waves before calling Jack. But first, he emailed his daughter, Jessica, asking her to call him when she had time. With her Kona Police Department contacts, she could look into Mr. Lau's criminal past in Hawaii.

Mike dialed Jack and got the answering machine. "Hey, Jack. Call me when you get back. I need to talk to you."

A few seconds later his phone rang. He hoped it was Jack on the other line, but it wasn't.

"Aloha, Mike speaking."

"Aloha, Mike, this is Kimo, returning your call. You left a message yesterday. You're interested in the dive boat I have for sale on Craigslist?"

"Yeah, is it still available?"

"It is, but I got one guy that says he's coming to look at it later this afternoon. But you know how that goes. If you want to check it out, I'll be here all day today."

"Where's the boat located?"

"Hilo," answered Kimo.

"Okay, text me your address, and I'll leave right now."

"Shoots, brah, I send'm."

Mike needed to replace the resort's dive boat right away because it had a blown engine. Every day the boat wasn't operating cost him income he couldn't afford to lose right now.

Kimo's boat was over ninety miles from Kona. Mike decided it was better to fly his plane to Hilo. That way he could get there faster and check it out before the other potential buyer got there. He got up from the picnic table and dialed Kona Air Services while walking across the beach back to his truck.

Kai Santos picked up the phone right away.

"Air Services, Kai speaking, how may I help you?"

"Howzit, Kai. Mike Murphy here. I need to banzai to Hilo real quick to check out a boat. Can you fuel my plane?"

"Shoots, brah, no problem. It will be ready to go by the time you get here."

"Mahalos, Kai." Mike hung up the phone and headed to the Kona airport.

On the way to the airport, Mike's truck got a flat on the highway, but he didn't have a lug wrench. He waited for an hour for someone to stop and help. That put him an hour behind schedule and in a huge rush to get to Hilo. He arrived at the airport and thanked Kai for getting his plane fueled.

Five minutes later, he was on the taxiway, waiting for clearance from the tower as the Gulfstream jet in front of him roared down the runway. In his haste, Mike skipped the preflight inspection of running up his plane's engine on the ramp. The plane had a fresh annual; there shouldn't be any problems. Famous last words.

Mike was on the runway when he heard through his headset, "November Hotel Juliet 224, cleared for takeoff."

"November Hotel Juliet 224 cleared for takeoff," Mike answered the controller and then applied full throttle and sped down the runway. The Beechcraft Bonanza lifted off and climbed above the lava field. At a little over three hundred feet, the engine died, and the plane stalled. There wasn't enough altitude to recover from the stall, and the small plane plunged straight into the lava rocks below. Mike Murphy died instantly in the crash.

Los Angeles

It was 2:12 a.m. when the phone on the nightstand rang. Jessica rolled over and grabbed it, squinting to see who was calling in the middle of the night. She was exhausted from the murder investigation she had just worked twenty hours straight to close. Jessica couldn't even focus one eye to read the screen on her phone. She opted to press the Off button and go back to sleep.

Twenty minutes later, Jessica heard two knocks—loud, like cops banging on the front door. "Crap. Go away," she grumbled.

She rolled out of bed, grabbed her .45 off the nightstand and stumbled to the front door. After a quick look through the peephole, she opened the door.

"Sorry to wake you, Lieutenant Kealoha, but the watch commander said it was important that we wake you up and tell you to call your sister in Hawaii. There's been an accident."

This wasn't good. She thanked the two burly street cops and closed the door.

Now wide awake from the adrenaline flowing through her veins, she picked up her cell phone and saw that her sister Pua was the one who called. She knew it must be serious. Pua never called her during the day, much less in the middle of the night. Jessica hit the redial on her phone as she paced the floor of her small apartment living room. Pua answered on the first ring.

"Jessica, there's been an accident," Pua said while sobbing.

"What happened, Pua?" Jessica asked softly.

"This morning Dad took off from the Kona airport and crashed his plane. He's dead. A witness said they heard the plane's engine sputter and quit, only a few hundred feet in the air. Then it crashed into the lava field, and Dad died on impact."

Jessica felt a sharp pain in the pit of her stomach, as if she had been kicked in the gut. Her knees buckled, and her eyes welled up with tears.

"I'll be on the first flight to Kona in the morning," Jessica said, in a complete daze.

After hanging up the phone, she sat on the couch, tired of pacing. She stared at a photo of her father hanging on the wall. Jessica was in total shock. For the first time in three years, she felt like taking a drink. But that was no longer an option for her. She took a second to think through what would happen if she had a drink. Her next thought was "maybe tomorrow, not today."

She couldn't believe it. Her father, of all people, dying in an airplane accident—it made little sense. He always took great care of his plane. He was a perfectionist when it came to maintenance. Her father had been an engineer on the inter-island cruise ship for twenty years before going into the hospitality business. Nobody took better care of their airplane than Dad did. He knew better than anyone that equipment failure always seemed to happen at the worst possible time.

Something just didn't add up. How could this have happened? Was it sabotage? Who would want to do this? Her father didn't have any enemies as far as she knew. Maybe it was just an accident. He had been running the Aloha Village at least ten years now. Jessica doubted anyone would want to kill him over something related to the resort.

Her mind raced. She needed answers.

2

GOING TO HAWAII

The flight from LAX to Kona took five hours and twenty-five minutes—a lot of time for Jessica to think. It was too soon to conclude that foul play had caused her father's death, but her gut told her there was something wrong. During most of the flight, Jessica wrote notes on her tablet about things she would do while back on the island.

As Jessica looked out the window of the 757 jet, the captain announced over the PA that they would land in Kailua-Kona in a few minutes. The turquoise ocean below, off the west side of the big island of Hawaii, was just as calm as a lake. It was typical of the leeward side of the island. The big island's beauty from the air was overwhelming, from the snow-covered tops of Mauna Kea and Mauna Loa to the extinct volcanoes of Kohala and Hualalai.

Jessica could see half a dozen fishing charters off the coast, most likely trolling for marlin. They reminded her of all the times she and her father would go fishing together. Just the thought of it caused her eyes to well up with tears. A minute later, she pushed those emotions back down, just like she always did when she saw a disturbing crime scene involving a child. The other thing she could see was the lava flow where her father had crashed his plane and lost his life.

As the big jet was on final approach over the lava flow, she said a prayer for her father. She didn't believe there was a God that cared one way or the other, but she figured it never hurt to hedge your bet, just in case. If there was one, he had a lot of explaining to do as far as she was concerned.

Jessica texted Pua after the plane landed and taxied to the gate. *I should be at the curb in a few minutes.*

As she exited the aircraft and walked down the ramp to the tarmac, she felt the warm, balmy breeze brush her cheeks. The smell of plumeria flowers nearby filled her nostrils. For a moment, she felt both sadness and relief at being back in Kona.

Kailua-Kona was a small town on the leeward side of the big island. The locals referred to it as a drinking town with a fishing problem. It had the best blue marlin fishing in the world, and it was hot and dry compared to the other side of the island, where Hilo, the county seat, was located.

Almost every day in Kona, it rained in the late afternoon above the eight-hundred-foot elevation. That also made it one of the best places in the world to grow coffee because of its unique weather pattern—early-morning sunshine and afternoon showers.

Pua had arrived at the airport a few minutes early—uncharacteristically, since she was always late. She waited for Jessica out front at the curb in her new red Mercedes SUV as she listened to Bruno Mars. She was texting her broker about a real estate deal on the verge of blowing up. The other agent involved in the transaction had misrepresented the facts to her buyer. Pua's seller had told them to go screw themselves once he'd figured out the truth because of something the buyer had said during a chance encounter with the seller.

Pua always went first class. Louie Vuitton handbags, Vera Wang dresses, and the most expensive perfumes. She didn't care if she only had two nickels to her name; she wanted you to think she was wealthy by all outward appearances. But Pua was your typical real estate agent, broke one day and rich the next. From the looks of the new SUV, she was making bank these days, at least until the next downturn in the economy. She was a grasshopper through and through and could be a real diva. The ability to look the part made her feel like a high-end realtor—fake it until you make it, that was her motto. Pua only handled properties over a million dollars.

Jessica was a jeans and T-shirt kind of girl and could never understand how Pua had come from the same gene pool. It was just one of life's little mysteries that she had yet to figure out. When Pua saw Jessica heading toward the SUV, she got out of the driver's seat and waved at Jessica. Pua was wearing Maui Jim sunglasses to hide her puffy eyes, a tank top, jogging shorts and rubber slippers.

Who are you and what have you done with my sister? Jessica thought when she saw Pua. Grief—everyone had different ways of handling it, as Jessica knew from experience. Jessica was so good at hiding her emotions that no one could tell what was going on with her unless she shared it. But anybody that knew Pua could take one look at her and know something was wrong in her world.

The two sisters had been ambivalent toward each other their whole lives. When they hugged behind the Mercedes after Jessica had stowed her carry-on bag, it felt like they meant it for the first time in their lives.

"Are you hungry, sis, or do you just want to go to the house?" Pua asked.

"I need a shower and some sleep," Jessica answered.

"Do you want to stay in my ohana, or do you want to go to Dad's?"

"I appreciate your offer. I may take you up on it later. But for now, I want to go to Dad's."

The sisters left the airport and headed north on the Queen

Ka'ahumanu Highway to their father's bungalow at Aloha Village Resort. Pua had Brother Iz playing softly in the background. The sisters were quietly lost in their thoughts. After about five minutes of silence between the two, Pua looked at Jessica

"You don't think he did it on purpose, do you?"

Jessica shook her head. "No. If he was still drinking, then I might consider that a possibility. Plus, I got an email from him before the accident."

"What did it say?"

"He asked me to call him and that it was urgent."

Pua looked at Jessica again. "Urgent?"

"He said he had a problem with a neighbor who wouldn't go away, and he wanted to talk about it."

"Mr. Lau," Pua muttered, shaking her head.

Jessica's eyes narrowed. "Mr. Lau?"

The SUV came to a stop. Pua had parked in front of their father's bungalow and turned off the engine.

"One day I was having lunch with Dad. His lawyer called, and Dad mentioned a Mr. Lau in the conversation. He was agitated when he got off the phone. He said the guy wanted to buy Aloha Village and kept making lowball offers. But Dad said hell would freeze over before he would sell it to that guy."

❀

PUA DROPPED Jessica off at their father's bungalow and promised to meet up later after Jessica had a little rest and a shower.

As Jessica walked up the stairs leading to the front door, she could feel his presence. Even though he wasn't there, she felt his spirit, and a warm feeling rushed over her as she walked through the front door. Jessica felt the mana to her core. The house was like he always kept it. Neat, but nothing fancy. It was typical Hawaiian style, with rattan wicker furniture and a canoe paddle hanging on the wall in the living room. The decor was an early vacation rental, except for the front door, which had a Mako shark carved into it. Since the mana of the shark was important in Hawaiian culture, her dad figured it was a good omen for the place.

Mike Murphy was a no-frills kind of guy who loved Hawaii and its culture. But the one thing in his life he'd spared no expense on was his starburst-blue '69 Road Runner with a 426 Hemi sitting in the garage. He called it the BOAT, which stood for Bust Out Another Thousand. He was always installing some expensive new speed part to make it faster. No doubt Mike Murphy was Kona's fastest grandpa. He was a racer at heart. It didn't matter what it was—cars, canoes, airplanes—he had to have a fast one.

The bungalow had two bedrooms and a huge bath with an emerald-green granite countertop and matching floor-to-ceiling tiles. Early Hawaiian garage sale was okay for the rest of the house, but you would have sworn the bathroom was from the presidential suite down the road at the Hilton. But unlike the Hilton, the bungalow's jalousie windows allowed the cool ocean breeze to circulate throughout the house, with a smell of salt in the air that Jessica could taste.

Jessica rolled her suitcase into the guest bedroom closet and fell backward on the bed. Too tired to put her things away, she wanted to take a nap before seeing her younger sister Jasmine. After lying there a few minutes, she realized something had been missing in the living room. Even though she was exhausted, the investigator in her forced her to get up off the bed and walk back into the living room. After taking a look around the room, she realized there were no photos of her mother anywhere in sight. Jessica thought it was strange but went back to bed and let it go until after she had some sleep.

❀

Jasmine was the youngest of the three sisters, and her father's right-hand man. He'd always thought of her that way, since boys had not been in the cards for the Murphy ohana. Jasmine ran Aloha Village for him when he was away. She had been at the beach all day, filling in for the lifeguard who'd called in sick.

The day before, a shark had swum in close to shore and hung out in the small bay for an hour before swimming away. No one had seen it since, but Jasmine had told all the resort's guests to stay out of the water for at least twenty-four hours.

Once satisfied the shark had left the area for good, Jasmine removed the shark signs from the beach. It was almost the last thing she had to do before going to see her older sister, Jessica. But first, she had to inform all the guests that they could go back into the water.

Grayson Roderick, a stockbroker and first-time guest visiting from California, thought someone should have killed the shark at the first sighting, so as not to interfere with his snorkeling plan for the day. He'd complained when Jasmine had informed him that wasn't happening. She'd kindly reminded him that the shark was in its natural habitat and that it was we who were encroaching. Mr. Roderick had grumbled something about going to Florida next time and walked away. Jasmine bit her tongue. She was always friendly and professional with the guests. Even the ones who should have been allowed to swim with the sharks.

Jasmine knocked on the door of her father's hale and waited. When Jessica didn't answer, she used her master key to open the door and stepped into the living room. Her father's golden retriever, Comet, waited behind Jasmine until she opened the door, then he shot around her and headed for the master bedroom to find his master.

Jasmine could hear the shower running in the back of the

house and yelled out to Jessica to make sure she didn't startle her sister.

"I'm in the shower. I'll be out in a minute," Jessica shouted back.

Jasmine was hungry and checked the fridge while waiting for her sister. As usual, there wasn't a thing to eat. Her father never kept food in the house. He always liked to go down to the resort's restaurant, the Marlin House, to eat and talk story with the guests. Comet came out of the bedroom and looked at Jasmine, perplexed. He didn't understand why Mike wasn't there.

Jessica came out a few minutes later with a towel wrapped around her and gave Jasmine a big hug and a kiss on the cheek. When Comet saw Jessica, he whined and jumped in the air, spinning in circles to let her know how much he missed her. It had been two years since the last time Jessica had been home. She reached down and scratched Comet's head behind his ears the way he loved it.

"How you doing, honey? Here, come sit by me on the couch." Jessica motioned to Jasmine. Comet thought the invitation included him too, and he jumped up on the couch.

Tears flowed down Jasmine's cheeks.

"I keep hoping this is a nightmare I'm trapped in and I'll wake up from it. It doesn't seem real, though. I never thought about Dad leaving us until he was much older, and certainly not by accident. Maybe shot by a jealous lover or something," said Jasmine, a grin on her face as she wiped the tears away. Jessica hugged Jasmine as tears streamed down her face too.

"Pua called me after she dropped you off and said she's taking care of all the arrangements for Dad. She'll be back here at six p.m. She also said she'd talk to you about something important later at dinner. I'll give you a heads-up. I think she's sick or something."

"One of my girlfriends I paddle with is a nurse at the Kaiser Clinic in town and acts weird now whenever she sees me. I sense something is going on with Pua, and my friend can't say anything because of privacy laws. I'm worried about her. Please ask her what's going on with her for me, would you?"

Jessica looked at Jasmine for a moment. "Let's not read anything into it. After I talk to Pua, I'll let you know what's up."

Jasmine stayed curled up on the couch next to Jessica like she had after their mother had died when she was very young. As Jessica softly stroked Jasmine's hair, she asked. "Where did the photos of Mom go?" Jessica had her arm around Jasmine's shoulder and could feel her muscles tense when she asked the question.

"Dad's girlfriend, Simmy. That's what happened. The woman's a complete nutjob if you ask me. She was jealous of Mom's photos and asked Dad to take them down. He refused. So one day, when he was out surfing, she did and wouldn't tell him where she hid them. I don't know what Dad saw in her. She was always accusing him of running around with other women."

Jasmine paused for a minute. "The woman was scary kind of jealous about Mom's photos. I think Dad was planning to quit seeing her but kept prolonging the inevitable drama that would surely follow once he told her goodbye."

Jessica lightly squeezed Jasmine's shoulder. "We'll find every last one of Mom's photos and put them back up. Now, let's hele-on down to the Marlin House and see what's up with Pua."

3

MARLIN HOUSE

That night, the three sisters met for dinner at the Marlin House, greeted by a breathtaking view of the ocean. The Marlin House was Hawaiian style to the max. It had a tiki on each side of the front door. The foyer showcased three blue marlins mounted high above on the wall outside the dining room. The biggest one was a world record holder and weighed over a thousand pounds.

Jasmine and Jessica arrived first and grabbed a table in the back of the restaurant. Jessica didn't like surprises, so she always sat with her back against the wall, and Jasmine didn't care either way. That night Brudda Robert was playing soft Hawaiian melodies on a twelve-string guitar, and his wife Lehua danced hula. It reminded Jessica of the Hawaiian music she had grown up with and how much she missed it after moving to the mainland years ago.

Twenty minutes later, Pua showed up late as usual with Kainoa, her twelve-year-old son. Born with autism, Kainoa was quite a handful sometimes. Pua didn't drink, but she had every reason to. Most of the time, Kainoa was pretty well behaved out in public, but once in a while he had outbursts of emotion characteristic of autism. People would stare. And

Pua would give them stink-eye right back with interest. She may have been a diva, but she was a good mother. Kainoa had played hard that day at school and decided he would lie down in the booth next to Auntie Jessica and go to sleep.

Aloha Village only had twelve bungalows and wasn't big enough to sustain the Marlin House restaurant alone. Besides the locals in town, a lot of the guests staying next door at the Ming mega-resort ate at the Marlin House too—much to the displeasure of the Chinese billionaire, Mr. Lau. The extra business was what allowed the boutique-sized resort to have its own restaurant.

Sam Stewart got up from his table across the room and walked over to offer his condolences to Mike Murphy's daughters. Sam was wearing khaki shorts and a Tommy Bahama shirt. His hair had a wisp of grey in it, and he had a scar on the side of his neck that a pirate would have been proud of.

Sam only knew Jasmine because she managed the Village, but he could see the resemblance in Pua and Jessica and was almost positive they were family.

"I heard the news down at the harbor earlier today. I'm so sorry for your family's loss. Mike Murphy had more aloha than anyone I know. Many people will miss him."

"Mahalo, Mr. Stewart. These are my sisters, Jessica and Pua," said Jasmine.

"Nice to meet you ladies. I'm just sorry it's under these circumstances."

Pua and Jessica nodded in agreement. Then they both shook Sam's hand.

"If there's anything I can do, let me know."

Then Sam Stewart walked back to his table and sat down to finish his dinner.

Pua looked at Jessica and Jasmine.

"Do you know who that guy is?"

"All I know is he stays here from early November to late

April, early May. But unlike a snowbird, he's from Southern California," said Jasmine.

Pua whispered, "He's one of the richest men in the world. He's the CEO of Stewart Industries and worth about seven billion dollars. I recall seeing him on the cover of *Stinking Rich* magazine not that long ago." The three sisters laughed.

Jasmine felt her phone vibrate in her pocket. She checked to see who called. There was a message.

"Crap, I have to go," Jasmine said. "The front desk clerk says there's a problem she needs me to handle. Someone's demanding to speak to the manager. I'll be back. Don't eat all the lilikoi pie without me." She smirked.

"No worries. I'm training for Ironman, so I can't have any right now," said Pua.

After Jasmine walked away and Jessica was sure she was out of earshot, Jessica turned to Pua. "Okay, cards on the table. Since when are you training for a triathlon, and what's going on with you?"

"What do you mean, Jess?"

"Jasmine told me earlier that she thought you might be sick and were keeping it from her. Are you okay?"

"I'm not training. I'm just not eating sugar anymore," Pua said, looking away for a moment.

Pua could never beat Jessica at poker. Her older sister knew all her tells—plus she was an expert interrogator. Jessica looked Pua straight in the eye. "You know lying to me is not a winning strategy, right?"

Pua stirred her coffee, looking down at the table for a minute before looking back up, her eyes full of tears.

"Jasmine is right. I have breast cancer. I found a lump about six weeks ago and just got the test results back three days ago."

Jessica reached across the table and held Pua's hand, caressing it. The tears welled up in Jessica's eyes too now. The waiter was approaching the table but made a U-turn when he saw the two of them crying and hugging each other.

"I know you and I haven't been close, but I have a favor to ask, Jess. And it's not an easy one either. I need you to take Kainoa if I die."

Jessica nodded, then said, "You know I'm not exactly mother material, right?"

"Yeah, I know, but he'll be fine with you. I'm not the mother of the year, and he's survived so far," said Pua.

They both laughed and wiped away their tears with a fresh pile of napkins Michael quietly brought to the table earlier.

"We have one more thing to talk about, Jess. You know how Dad was a great engineer?" Pua asked.

Jessica took a deep breath and exhaled, sensing the bad news wasn't over yet.

"Yeah."

"The other side of the coin is he was never great at being a businessman. He always felt sorry for people, and he made bad business decisions over the last five years. Because he had too big of a heart, the bottom line is, Aloha Village is almost broke."

"Yeah, well, let's sell it," said Jessica.

"We can't. I called Dad's attorney to get the ball rolling, and he said there's a problem. But he wouldn't elaborate on the phone. He said if we come to his office tomorrow, he'll explain the situation. But I can't go—I have to get together with a client tomorrow. I can't get out of it. Some rich guy who's only on the island for one day and wants to see a house I've been trying to sell for almost two years. I can't blow him off. The potential deal is too important. Besides, if I close this deal, I'll make enough money for you to take care of Kainoa until he's an adult if I die."

Jessica knew Pua always had a flair for the dramatic, but

this time the danger was real, and she agreed to see the lawyer herself the next day.

JESSICA SAT in the waiting room of the Kona law office alone, waiting for her dad's lawyer to return from lunch. The secretary said he should be back any minute. Jessica passed the time by looking at photos of her and her father on her phone, taken on her last trip to Kona. She thought about the conversation they'd had about her moving back to Kona someday, after she retired from the LAPD.

She snapped back to the here and now as Mr. Jennings walked through the office door. He was short, fat and about two hundred years old. Just like Pua had said.

He hobbled into the room and motioned her to follow him into his office and have a seat in the dark leather chair. Between the two of them was a big mahogany desk with a stack of papers, which the old lawyer picked up and shuffled through to find Mike Murphy's will.

"Are Pua and Jasmine coming?" Mr. Jennings asked Jessica.

"No, Pua's too busy with some big real estate deal and Jasmine has to run the resort, so it's just going to be me and you today."

"Jessica, your father left you, Pua, and Jasmine the Aloha Village Resort. He didn't leave much cash to go with it. He had all his money tied up in the infrastructure of the property, and it's on the verge of bankruptcy. The good news is, your father controlled the master lease on the land underneath the resort. Selling it won't be a problem when the time comes, if you want.

"But there's a catch. If you and your sisters want to sell the resort, you'll have to renew the master lease first. That's the only way you'll get any money out of it. Mr. Lau, the owner of the Ming Resort next door, has made three lowball offers to buy the Village. He knew your father was near bankrupt. And he also knew the landowner trust wouldn't renew the master lease of the property if your father didn't bring the resort's buildings up to code.

"Your father wouldn't sell to Mr. Lau at any price because he knew he would ruin the Village. Your father viewed the island as sacred and fought to preserve it."

"Mr. Jennings, I have one question. Why didn't my father renew the lease now?"

"He didn't have enough money to make the infrastructure improvements the landowner required before they would renew. Your father could have borrowed the money, but he didn't want to be owing anything to anybody. Instead he was doing the improvements piecemeal as he had the money. He could be so stubborn sometimes," said Mr. Jennings.

Jessica smiled. "You're singing to the choir, Mr. Jennings. My father's middle name should have been stubborn."

"In the last few years, your father had become a fierce adversary of mainland developers who came to the island and tried to turn it into Waikiki. Your father's guests at the Village loved him. Real estate developers hated him with a passion because he turned up at every county council meeting and fought them every step of the way. He wasn't going to let them pour concrete over paradise without a fight. I'm sure there's a long list of real estate developers that are glad your father is no longer around to fight them," said Mr. Jennings.

"Why does this Mr. Lau want to buy the property so bad?" Jessica asked.

"For one reason, its beach. The Ming's beach is full of lava rocks. If the Ming can take over your father's property, they can use the Aloha Village beach and bulldoze the rest of the place.

"And there is one more thing." The old lawyer leaned

back in his chair. "Something you should know about Mr. Lau. He's a Chinese billionaire from Macau, and he's been buying property all over Hawaii the last couple of years. I suspect he would like to turn the Ming and Aloha Village into a casino if gambling ever gets legalized here. He owns half the casinos in Macau and is looking to expand his gambling empire to Hawaii, from the news articles I've read."

Mr. Jennings sat straight up in his chair and looked Jessica in the eye. "He's connected to the Triads is what I've heard on the coconut wireless, so be very careful with this guy."

Jessica left the law office on a mission. Investigating Mr. Lau would be her new job while she waited for the NTSB report to come back with the cause of the crash. Mr. Lau had a motive, a means, and a good reason to want her father dead. If Jessica knew one thing for sure, there were people in this world that would kill for any reason to get what they want. And Mr. Lau had millions of them. If it turned out Mike Murphy's plane crash had been the result of sabotage instead of an accident, he would be the prime suspect.

It was time to call Uncle Jack to see what he knew about this Mr. Lau.

4

MARLIN FISHING

After Jessica left Mr. Jennings's office, she drove out to the harbor to see if Uncle Jack was on his boat, the small fishing yacht he'd been living on since he'd retired. He wasn't answering his cell phone, as usual. Jessica knew he had gone to Hong Kong earlier in the month, but she thought he should be back by now.

Uncle Jack had the connections to find out information she couldn't about Mr. Lau. Even though Jessica hadn't talked to Uncle Jack yet, she knew without asking that he'd be deep into the investigation of his brother's death by now. Uncle Jack, suspicious by nature, came from the Ronald Reagan school of "trust but verify."

Uncle Jack had retired from the Naval Investigation Service unit at Pearl Harbor. His life now pretty much consisted of going fishing and keeping an eye on Kiki and Koa, two dolphins trained by the Navy for special ops. The dolphins had come from a pod off the Kona coast of the big island of Hawaii before the Navy had trained them for special ops. After closing down its dolphin program in Hawaii, the Navy had returned them to the area and released them back into the wild.

Since Jack Murphy had a top-secret security clearance, the Navy had asked him to keep an eye on them, which consisted of monitoring their location via the GPS tracking devices the Navy had implanted in them. Little did the Navy know, Jack used Kiki and Koa to help him catch fish. When word got out, it kept Jack's charter business as busy as he wanted.

Jessica pulled up to the slip of the *Hui Hou*, Uncle Jack's thirty-five-foot Cabo. It surprised her to find Uncle Jack and Sam Stewart sitting in the cockpit drinking beer. What was going on here? But Kona was a small town; it wouldn't be unusual if they were friends or something. Maybe they'd gone fishing. Uncle Jack wasn't the only one in the family that was suspicious by nature. That was a trait that made them both such good investigators.

The *Hui Hou* had just come in from a half-day trip down to Red Hill to troll for marlin. Jessica checked herself in the mirror and touched up her lip gloss before getting out of the 4Runner. She walked towards the slip of the *Hui Hou* and waved at Uncle Jack and Sam as she approached the boat.

Jessica smiled and gave Uncle Jack a big hug and then gave Sam one too. On the mainland, she would never have hugged Sam, but in Kona, it was the local style to hug even acquaintances in most social settings.

"Long time no see, Uncle," said Jessica.

"Well, that wouldn't be the case if you would move back to Kona," Uncle Jack said sarcastically. Sarcasm was Jack's specialty. Most of the time, he meant it in a good way. Unless he didn't like you. Then he had a whole special brand of it.

"Did you guys go fishing today, or just drink beer and talk story?"

"Sam caught Old Smokey, but he got off the line. Just like he always does. Grab something to drink out of the cooler. There's plenty of stuff in there besides beer," said Uncle Jack.

Jessica opened the cooler and grabbed a can of cold Japanese green tea. She popped the top open and took a sip.

Sam looked perplexed. "You mean that fish had a name?"

"Yeah, as soon as he jumped out of the water, I could tell it was Old Smokey by the big chunk missing out of his fin, right next to the tag. I also knew you had a snowball's chance in hell of reeling him to the boat. Many a fisherman in Kona has tried to reel Smokey in, and none have succeeded. Except for one guy," said Uncle Jack.

"Who's was that?" Sam asked.

"My brother, Mike. He tagged Smokey and let him go."

There was a silence among the three for a moment, and Sam lifted his beer towards Jack and Jessica. "To Mike Murphy." And the three of them toasted.

"Jack, I had a great time fishing with you today. And, Jessica, it was a nice surprise to see you again. I have to head back to Aloha Village."

Sam shook hands with Jack and hugged Jessica. But this time there was something electric when they embraced. They both felt it. And they both tried to ignore it. Before getting in his rental car, Sam walked over to a plumeria tree and plucked a red blossom off a low-hanging limb. He walked back over to the *Hui Hou* and handed it to Jessica, smiling, then turned and walked down the dock towards the parking lot. Jessica placed the flower above her left ear and thanked Sam as he was walking away.

"Interesting," said Uncle Jack. Jessica smiled like she hadn't in a long time and ignored Uncle Jack. But there was something about Sam that drew Jessica to him whether she wanted to admit it or not.

🌀

"ARE YOU READY FOR COFFEE? I picked up a fresh bag of roasted Makua. It's excellent," Uncle Jack said.

"Sure, why not?"

"Follow me inside to the galley. I'll grind it up, and we can talk story."

When Jack opened the bag of fresh Kona coffee beans, the aroma filled the galley and saloon of the *Hui Hou*. Jessica and Uncle Jack both breathed in deep and sighed almost in unison as they enjoyed the heavenly fragrance.

In the galley, Uncle Jack glanced at Jessica and asked, "What's on your mind?"

"Earlier today, I went to see Dad's attorney concerning his estate." Jessica took a seat at the breakfast bar and sat up straight on the stool, watching Uncle Jack grind the coffee beans. "He told me some things that make me think we need to take a closer look at Dad's death. Are you familiar with Mr. Lau at the Ming next to the Village?"

Uncle Jack nodded, pouring water into the coffeemaker. "Yes, he's been on my radar for a while."

"I don't suppose your trip to Hong Kong had anything to do with him, did it?" Jessica asked.

"I can't talk about it."

"I'll take that as a yes, then."

Uncle Jack pretended he didn't hear her and kept fussing about in the galley until the coffee was ready. Jessica moved to the couch. Uncle Jack followed with the coffee and sat next to her. Turning toward her, he looked her straight in the eye.

"I can tell you one thing for sure—my brother was anal about his airplane maintenance. The chances of him crashing due to a mechanical failure or pilot error are almost zero in my book. It's possible that's what happened. But I doubt it." Jack stared into his cup of coffee. "When do you go back to LA?"

"I'm here only until the paddle out, and then I have to go back and finish working a case."

"Do you still have contacts in the Kona PD?"

Jessica nodded. "Most of them I don't trust. But I have one I do."

Uncle Jack finished the last sip of his coffee and stood up to take his cup to the galley. "Keep their number handy. We may need them. The last contact I had there retired."

❀

BUNGALOW NUMBER seven sat on the edge of the beach. It had the best view of the ocean of all the bungalows at Aloha Village. Sam walked in and headed straight for the refrigerator, grabbing a cold beer. With beer and cell phone in hand, he went out front to the lanai, sat down on the chaise lounge and leaned back. He took a swig and looked out at the ocean, relaxing while going over what just happened at the harbor with Jessica.

It had been a great day of fishing on the *Hui Hou* with Jack Murphy. But meeting Jessica again had been the highlight of Sam's day. He loved her exotic look. Half Japanese on her mother's side and half everything else on her father's, otherwise known as hapa Hawaiian. She was one of the most beautiful women Sam had ever seen. At first, he'd thought he should put his feelings aside and wait for a more opportune time to pursue a relationship. But then he realized life was short, and there was no time to waste.

Sam didn't know Jack Murphy; they'd only met once before because of Mike. Mike had talked about his brother working for the Navy as an investigator. But that was all Sam knew, other than that Jack had retired, moved to Kona and started a charter business.

Sam had hoped he would learn more about Mike's death during the fishing trip. But Jack always played his cards close to the vest and didn't give up anything, so Sam wasn't too surprised. It had been worth a try. Not to mention, Sam had damn near caught a grander.

The story about Mike Murphy's airplane crashing on takeoff was all over the news. They all said it was an accident.

Almost everyone who knew Mike suspected it wasn't. Even though Mike was in the hospitality business, he had made a lot of enemies over the years fighting developers from the mainland. Sam added his name to the list of nonbelievers and wanted to help the family in any way he could to find the truth.

Sam picked up his cell phone from the table and dialed his assistant in California. She answered on the first ring.

"Hi, Melissa, it's Sam, I'm coming back next week like I planned. But I'm not staying long."

"Oh? Is there anything you would like me to take care of before you arrive, sir?"

"Yes, put the house in Newport Beach on the market. It's time. I'll be coming to pick up the things I want from the house, and Mr. Jangles. If it were just the stuff, I'd ship it, but I'm not shipping the cat," Sam said.

"Anything else?" Melissa asked.

"Yes, donate all of Jamie's things."

Melissa didn't want to ask, but she knew she had to. "Are you sure?"

"I'm sure," Sam said without hesitation. He'd never liked the Newport house much, but it had been Jamie's favorite, and he hadn't been ready to let it go until now.

Sam had just been going through the motions these last few years, staying busy with the day-to-day operations of his global empire. It had been five years since Jamie's death, and Sam had been alone all that time. He'd had no interest in other women until he'd met Jessica.

THE NEXT MORNING, Sam lay in bed listening to the sound of the ocean and the chorus of exotic Hawaiian birdsong outside his bungalow. He propped his head up with two pillows and looked out at the ocean. The sea breeze flowed through the bedroom through the open sliding glass door, and he could hear the waves crashing on the beach outside. After the nine minutes of meditation he always did first thing in the morning, he thought about his plans for the day. First, he'd take a morning swim in the ocean, and then he'd eat breakfast at the Marlin House.

When Sam walked in the front door of the restaurant, he headed towards his usual table in the corner. It surprised him to see Jessica already sitting there, sipping tea. Sam walked right up and sat down as if they had planned to meet. Jessica had her head buried in the newspaper, engulfed in a story about the Hawaii reefs dying from the effects of global warming, and didn't even notice Sam had sat down. When she looked up, their brown eyes met, and Jessica peered into Sam's for a moment as if two long-lost souls had reconnected.

Jessica said nothing. Sam smiled and said, "Good morning. I'll move to another table in a moment. I sit here every morning, but it's obvious you got here first. Unless you're willing to share?"

Jessica smiled back and then continued reading the paper.

"I'll take that as a yes," Sam said as he picked up a menu. He didn't need to read it. He had it memorized and ordered the same thing for breakfast every morning. But he figured he'd hide his face in it until he could think of what his next move would be.

That morning, Momi was serving tables and walked up to their table.

"Good morning, Mr. Stewart. Mahi-mahi and eggs as usual?"

"That would be great, Momi."

Momi disappeared back to the kitchen to put in Sam's request.

"Good thing you studied the menu," Jessica said as she folded the paper and set it down on the table. Her brown eyes looked straight at Sam, and she asked, "You knew my father well?"

"I did. We were good friends. We both liked boats and muscle cars. Your father and I would sit down at the Castaway bar and talk story for hours about who had the faster car or canoe. And this whole thing just makes little sense."

Jessica nodded in agreement.

"I'd like to help you find out the truth of what happened to your father in any way I can. While I'm not an investigator like you are, I do have something to contribute," Sam said.

Jessica's eyebrows rose a little. She wondered how he knew she was an investigator. She doubted Uncle Jack would have told him. Hmmm, maybe Jasmine.

Sam noticed Jessica's surprise and added, "Your father mentioned it a few times. That's how I knew."

"Sam, I appreciate your offer, but I work best alone."

Sam wasn't used to people telling him no. He thought for a moment and then asked, "Does that apply to your personal life too?"

"What makes you think I'm alone?"

Jessica took a sip of her tea as Loana came to the table with Sam's breakfast. Sam sliced into his fish, and just before taking a bite, he said, "No wedding ring. And I asked one of my spies here at the resort." Sam smiled as he chewed his fish.

The coconut wireless was one thing Jessica didn't miss when she was in LA. There were no secrets in Kona. Everyone knew everyone, and they all seemed to know each other's business. Jessica didn't miss that one bit.

"What do you think about having dinner?" Sam asked.

"I have it most nights," Jessica answered, grinning.

"I mean us," Sam said with all the courage he could muster. This was difficult for him, and she wasn't going to make it any easier.

"It was nice to see you again, Mr. Stewart." Jessica stood

up from the table to leave. "I'm sure you're a nice man, but I don't have time right now to get sidetracked. I have to find out what happened to my father." She grabbed her sunglasses off the table and walked out the front door of the Marlin House.

Sam couldn't believe he had just been shot down over what he thought was friendly territory. This just didn't compute. Women threw themselves at Sam all the time. He was the heartbreaker. Not the other way around. *Game on*, Sam thought.

5

PADDLE OUT

As she made the short walk back up the hill to Mike's bungalow, Jessica thought about Sam. She felt something there and wanted to explore that feeling more. But her priority was to handle her father's estate and find out the truth about his death. As she walked up to the bungalow, she saw a car parked in the driveway, and the front door was open. It appeared as if someone was loading the car with things from the bungalow. Jessica walked in the front door with a fair amount of caution and came face-to-face with Simmy, who was attempting to carry a painting out the door. It was her father's favorite and had been in the family since Jessica was a child. Her father had gotten it on a trip to Japan, when he'd met Jessica's mother for the first time.

Jessica had met Simmy before and wasn't a fan. "Put it down, leave, and don't come back or I'll have you arrested for trespassing," said Jessica.

"Listen, bitch—"

Before Simmy could say another word, Jessica stepped behind her, grabbed her right wrist and swung it behind her back. She had Simmy by the neck and pushed her out the front door, just like she'd done a thousand times taking people to jail. Jessica slammed the door behind her as if she had just taken the trash out. Simmy got in her car and left in a cloud of burning rubber, spewing profanities out the window as she sped off.

Jessica then called Jasmine. "Hi, honey, is Jason still the handyman?"

"Yes," Jasmine answered.

"Send him up to Dad's place and have him change all the locks. Today."

"I'll send him right up."

Jessica decided she would fly back to LA as soon as possible and put in her retirement papers. There was no way she could leave Jasmine and Pua alone to deal with Simmy and run Aloha Village. And Pua would need her support while she battled breast cancer.

Cousin Jason was full-blooded Hawaiian and a jack of all trades at Aloha Village. Not only was he the resort handyman during the day, but he was also the fire knife dancer at the Friday night luau. It was a good thing, since he'd almost burned the stage down during the show once. He had flung the torch too high and it had landed on the stage's thatch roof. It had taken him two days to repair the damage.

Five minutes later, Jason knocked on the front door. Jessica opened the door and hugged him.

"Good to see you again, cuz," she said.

"You too, Auntie," he answered. "Jasmine said you want me to change the locks. Should I be on the lookout for anyone suspicious?"

"If you see Simmy, call the cops, and then me," said Jessica.

"You got it. I never liked that tita much anyways."

❀

MIKE MURPHY'S will stated that when the day came, there

would be no memorial service on land. Instead, there'd be a paddle out, and his ashes would be scattered at sea. And just as he wished, about two hundred and fifty people met at Kohanaiki Beach Park on a beautiful Saturday morning. At nine a.m., they all paddled out about two hundred yards offshore to spread Mike's ashes. Jessica, Pua, Jasmine, and Kainoa sat on their surfboards in the inner circle, floating in the sea like one big plumeria lei, surrounded by over two hundred people.

Afterward, there was a celebration in honor of Mike's life on the beach. No speeches, just people were hanging out, grilling ono grinds and talking story about good times they'd had with Mike.

An hour later, a black stretch limo pulled into the parking lot near the beach. Two men got out of the car and walked down to the main tent on the beach to sign the guestbook and pay their respects to the family. The older man was Mr. Lau, the owner of the Ming Resort. He was in his late sixties and wore a five-thousand-dollar suit. It was obvious he hadn't gotten the memo this was a casual affair—or he didn't care.

Mike Murphy's family sat in the main tent and talked story with all the folks who had come to sign the guestbook and pay their respects. Pua knew Mr. Lau and introduced him to Jessica and Uncle Jack. They all shook hands and were cordial to each other. Except for Woo Ching who stood silently off to the side and glared at everybody. But Mr. Lau showing up had little to do with paying respects. The gloves would come off soon enough on both sides.

After Mr. Lau and Woo Ching were on their way back to the limo and out of earshot, Jessica whispered to Uncle Jack. "Who was the creepy guy with Mr. Lau?"

"Funny you should ask that. I ran him through Interpol when he first showed up here a few months ago. His name is Woo Ching, and he's Mr. Lau's nephew. He's also connected to the Triads in Hong Kong, and he has a rap sheet as long as your leg. He's a real nice boy," Uncle Jack said sarcastically.

"I don't suppose your recent trip to Hong Kong had anything to do with him."

Before Uncle Jack could answer, Sam walked up and greeted everyone.

Uncle Jack stood and said he had to get ready for a trip back to Hong Kong. He put his hand on Jessica's shoulder and told her to have a nice trip if he didn't see her again before she returned to the mainland.

"No worries, Uncle. I'm coming back. I have to put in my retirement papers and clear out my apartment. Then I'll be back to help Pua and Jasmine."

Uncle Jack looked perplexed. "I thought you had to finish working a case."

"It's obvious my family needs me more than the LAPD," answered Jessica.

The sudden revelation stunned everyone. Even cousin Jason, who was playing his ukulele, stopped strumming for a moment. No one had ever expected Jessica to move back to Kona.

Sam's eyes lit up, and he had to concentrate to contain his excitement. "Do you need a ride to LA?" he asked.

Jessica looked at Sam, puzzled.

"I'm going to LA myself, and I have a plane here," Sam explained.

"That's very generous, Sam, but I'm fine with the red-eye," said Jessica.

"We can leave at night if that'll make you feel better," Sam said. Everyone laughed. Even Jessica, who was always too serious. And to sweeten the deal, Sam said, "No TSA, and no long lines to wait in to board the plane."

Uncle Jack put his hand on Jessica's shoulder and whispered in her ear, "Sam is a good man. Accept his offer, and I'll tell you about Hong Kong when you get back."

"Okay, Uncle."

Uncle Jack smiled, hugged Pua and Jasmine and then left to go pack for his trip to Hong Kong.

Jessica didn't want to give Sam the wrong idea; she still wasn't interested in a relationship. Not because she didn't like Sam, but because she was on a mission to find out what happened to her father. After that, who knew? Maybe she would think about Sam.

"Okay, Sam, I'd love to hitch a ride. When do you plan on leaving?"

"How about tomorrow morning? The plane is always ready to go. Meet me at Air Service at about ten a.m.?"

Private jets and traveling on a whim wasn't the world Jessica lived in, but it sure sounded inviting. Putting in her retirement papers would be bittersweet after twenty-one years on the force. And moving back to Kona could be just the thing to fill the void in her life.

🐚

THE NEXT MORNING, Jasmine drove Jessica to the airport. When they pulled into the parking lot, Sam was already there, standing out front of the office next to the Air Services shuttle, talking with Kai Santos, the FBO manager.

Jessica hugged Jasmine. "I'll be back in a week." Jasmine beamed a big smile, nodded, and then drove away.

"Howzit, Jessica," Kai said. "Long time no see."

Kai knew Jessica from high school. They'd both attended Konawaena at the same time. "Aloha, Kai, you look good."

"It's from canoe paddling," Kai said.

Sam opened the side door of the van and motioned to Jessica. "After you."

Kai drove Sam and Jessica out to the Gulfstream jet on the ramp and wished them a safe trip. As they walked up the short staircase of the G650, Sam placed his hand on the small of Jessica's back. His touch sent a warm feeling up and down her spine, something she hadn't felt for a long time.

Once on board, Captain Mike Johnson stood in the doorway next to the cockpit and greeted Sam and Jessica. "Good morning, Mr. Stewart. Good morning, ma'am."

"Good morning, Captain. This is Ms. Kealoha." Jessica smiled and shook hands with Captain Johnson.

"Winds are light today. Flight time is five hours and four minutes, sir," Captain Johnson said.

"Giddy up, Captain."

The Gulfstream jet climbed out of Kona, making a right turn over the ocean as it headed towards the US mainland.

Jessica sat buckled into the soft leather chair next to Sam and looked around the cabin. *So this is what it's like to be a member of the wealthiest one percent.*

"If you want to take a nap, there's a button on the side of the chair that will recline your seat flat, converting it into a bed," Sam said.

"I'd like that. I didn't get much sleep last night." Twenty minutes later, she was asleep, and Sam got a blanket out of the closet to cover her.

Sam had hoped he would get to know Jessica better on the flight to California. But she slept the whole trip and didn't awake until they landed at John Wayne Airport in Orange County. It was the first time she had slept over three hours in a row since her father's death. Jessica felt safe with Sam, which allowed her to sleep.

Security was always a concern when Sam was anywhere else in the world besides Kona. And because of that, after landing, Captain Johnson taxied to Sam's private hangar. That way, Sam and Jessica could depart without the prying eyes of the tabloids' mercenary photographers. The last thing Sam wanted was to have Jessica scrutinized in the press. That was one thing Sam loved about living in Kona part-time—the anonymity that came with it. Nobody cared what you did on the mainland or how famous you were there.

Inside the hangar were two black Ford Expeditions with dark-tinted windows, each with a driver standing nearby. "The driver will take you anywhere you want to go." Sam handed Jessica a piece of paper. "This is my contact info. If you need anything, just get in touch."

As instructed, the driver took Jessica to her apartment in Anaheim, just a few miles from Disneyland. Jessica didn't care for Anaheim, but she liked going to Disneyland a few times a month since it was the happiest place on earth. It was a nice contrast to the ugliness she witnessed investigating murders every day at work.

IT HAD BEEN a busy week for Jessica. She had put in her papers, said her goodbyes, and packed up her apartment. There was nothing left to do except go back to Kona, and she caught the afternoon United flight out of LAX. She thought about calling Sam to get a ride back but decided it might give him the wrong idea.

The funny thing about Kona was that it was such a small town, it wasn't unusual to see people you knew on the plane. Even though Jessica had been away for many years, she'd been born and raised in Kona and still knew many people there. While sitting in the lounge, waiting to board the plane, Jessica recognized Sonny Palio. Their eyes met at the same time, and it was obvious he recognized her too. Annoyed with herself for not looking away sooner, she now felt oblig-ated to talk with him when he beelined over to strike up a conversation. He was an old boyfriend, and as they chatted, it became evident why their relationship had never gone past high school. The conversation went something like, "Now that you know what I think about me, what do you think about me?" What had she been thinking back then? Hormones were the only rational explanation.

After boarding the plane, she sat about sixteen rows away and tried not to look in his direction for the entire flight. He stopped by her seat to chat once more while he was on the way to the bathroom and said they should get together in Kona. Ugh. Did that mean for coffee, or did he think they should get back together as in dating? Men were funny; you never knew what was going through their brains. But most of the time it had something to do with their penis, she thought.

That was one thing she'd miss about the big city: the anonymity that came with it. Going to the store and not recognizing a soul—there was comfort in that sometimes. But right now, her family needed her more than ever. She would have to put her personal preferences aside for the time being.

SAM HAD ALSO BEEN VERY busy. He'd signed the documents for the sale of the Newport house and was ready to move on with his life after five years of being alone.

Sam had his businesses set up to run by themselves. He liked setting them up, but he didn't care to run them from day to day. Sam would always find a key employee to take over. And when possible, he would pick one who came from the humblest of backgrounds. Sam just liked helping people succeed. The next business Sam wanted to set up was an interisland ferry system.

Sam had always lived near the ocean and felt a connection to it. The next step would be to call the governor to arrange a meeting to see if he would smooth the regulatory process. Hawaii was just like any other place; it wasn't always what you knew, it was who you knew. The backroom deal was alive and well in the Aloha State.

Sam called Melissa. "I need you to call the governor of Hawaii's office and set up a meeting."

"What should I tell him it's about?" asked Melissa.

"I want to start an interisland ferry. And I would prefer not to spend five years in court with the conservationists before getting started."

"I'll take care of it and let you know when I have a date for the meeting," said Melissa.

Sam had one more phone call to make. "Hey, Mike, it's Sam. Meet me at the airport tomorrow morning at ten. It's time to go back to Kona."

"Ten a.m. tomorrow. Roger that," Mike said.

It bummed Sam out he never heard from Jessica during the week they were on the mainland. But he was patient, and he knew they would be together in due time. Now all he needed to do was convince her of that.

6

RETURN TO KONA

As soon as Jessica landed in Kona, she turned her phone on and it pinged with a dozen text messages. One of them was from Uncle Jack. "We have to talk." Rather cryptic, she thought.

Six hours earlier, before boarding the plane, Jessica had called Pua and asked if she could pick her up at the airport. Pua had agreed and said she'd be parked at the curb in front of the airport. Instead, it was Jasmine.

"Where's Pua?" Jessica asked as she put her suitcase in the trunk of Jasmine's Kona cruiser, a yellow '85 Toyota Tercel.

"She's sick. She asked me to come get you," said Jasmine. Jessica's momentary annoyance evaporated, and guilt took its place.

Jessica asked Jasmine to drive straight to the harbor first so she could see Uncle Jack. When they arrived at the slip, the *Hui Hou* wasn't there. He must still be out on a charter, Jessica thought. As they were getting ready to leave, the *Hui Hou* came into the harbor. Uncle Jack and another man Jessica didn't recognize were the only ones on board.

After the boat docked, the man left the *Hui Hou* with a bag full of mahi-mahi and a smile so big you'd need a crowbar to pry it off his face.

Jessica asked Jasmine to sit in the car and said she'd be back in a few minutes. Jasmine was content with that, since she'd be able to resume texting with a guy she'd met online the day before and was planning to meet for a drink later.

"Hey, Uncle. I got your text," Jessica said as she walked up to the boat. Uncle Jack was washing the deck.

"Where's Sam?" he asked with a curious look on his face.

"California? I don't know. It's not my day to watch him. Anyway, what's up?" Said Jessica.

Uncle Jack looked down at the deck as he rinsed it with the freshwater garden hose from the dock. Then he looked up and said, "Did you see that guy that left the boat?"

Jessica nodded.

"He's the lead NTSB investigator assigned to your dad's crash. His name's Derek Higashi. I've got a friend in the FAA who knows him. He got me an off-the-record phone call with him, which led to an off-the-record day of deep sea fishing on the *Hui Hou*. He found sugar in the gas tank of your dad's airplane. The sugar plugged up the fuel filter, which prevented the engine from getting fuel and caused the loss of power that resulted in the crash."

Jessica could feel her anger boil. She gritted her teeth. "We'll find out who did this, and they'll pay."

Jack nodded. "Let's keep this to ourselves for now. The NTSB report won't come out for months. We might as well use that to our advantage and figure out who did this before they're even aware we're looking for them."

"Agreed," Jessica said.

Uncle Jack and Jessica had both started out in law enforcement in Kona. They knew there was a fine line between the cops and the criminals on the island. Some Kona families had their fair share of both—including the Murphy ohana.

"I'm doing a contract job for Homeland Security right now

because of my extensive contacts in Hong Kong. The Tongs and yakuza operating in Hawaii and California never worried the feds too much, but the Triads gaining a foothold in Hawaii scares the FBI and Homeland Security. The Triads are serious gangsters with ties to the Chinese government. What's interesting about this is that the Triads have never operated out of Asia—until now. There's more to it—it's classified, but let's just say it's related to the Chinese government.

"I can't go any anywhere near Mr. Lau. My boss says he's off-limits. Hell, I don't know why. I have my suspicions, though. So you'll have to see if you can interview him. I'll work the back channels and do what I can to help, but you'll be the lead dog on this Jessica," Uncle Jack said.

A car horn sounded, and they turned to see Jasmine leaning out the window of her old Tercel. "Eh! I got places to go," she called out.

Jessica held up her index finger and turned back to Jack. "Okay, Uncle, I get um," Jessica said with the tone of pidgin that meant business.

Jessica and Jasmine threw Uncle Jack a shaka, and they left the harbor and headed back to Aloha Village. Jasmine had a hot date with a guy she would meet at the bar at the Ming. And Jessica had a hot date with the bathtub at her dad's place. An hour soaking in the tub thinking about what Uncle had Jack said was the next step.

THE FOLLOWING DAY at the Marlin House, Sam arrived half an hour early to claim his table. Like most people, Sam was a creature of habit and liked having a morning ritual. The rest of the day, he could wing it. But mornings were sacred to him, and he wanted things just so. Sam reserved his bungalow at Aloha Village for another two weeks, and then he would move to his yacht, *The Racer*, which was en route to Kona so he would have a place to stay while he looked for a house to buy.

Jessica's favorite table at the Marlin House was the one where Sam always sat. But she wouldn't do what he had done last time. No, she'd pick a different spot to sit and get to work thinking only about the next step in the investigation. A seaside romance was the last thing on her mind.

Before sitting down at the other side of the restaurant, she stopped by Sam's table and thanked him for the ride to California and the car service.

Sam reiterated that if there was anything he could do to help find out what had happened to Mike, she should let him know. Jessica thanked him for his offer but politely conveyed that she doubted he could help. She was the homicide cop. He was the rich guy. What could he bring to the table?

Sam had finished his breakfast and was sipping his coffee and taking in the view of the ocean from his table when his cell phone buzzed. "Hello?" Sam answered.

"It's Melissa. I got you an appointment to meet Governor Fitch on Thursday at nine a.m. It so happens he was coming to Kona that day to play golf at the Ming. He said he could meet you there at the clubhouse for a few minutes before his tee time."

Sam wasn't too surprised at Fitch's willingness to meet so soon. Hawaii was the "You scratch my back, I'll scratch yours" state. The governor knew Sam wanted something, and he also knew Sam would contribute sizably to his reelection campaign if the governor could give him what he wanted. That was one great thing about being a billionaire; people always took your phone calls.

Before Sam left the Marlin House, he walked over to Jessica's table. "I'm meeting with the governor on Thursday at the Ming if you'd like to tag along. He might be of some help with your father's accident investigation."

Jessica had a mouth full of loco moco and couldn't talk,

but she nodded. And then Sam walked away just as fast as he had approached the table.

Jessica didn't have any desire to meet the governor, but she sure as hell wanted to go next door to the Ming and chat with Mr. Lau. Maybe Sam could be useful after all.

That night she called Sam to confirm that she would love to go with him to the Ming on Thursday.

🍥

SAM PICKED Jessica up Thursday morning at 8:30 and they shared a golf cart ride over to the Ming next door. They hadn't crossed paths the last couple of days because Sam had been out with Pua, looking at properties to buy. He liked staying at Aloha Village, but it wasn't a long-term solution. If he moved to Kona, he would buy a place.

"Pua showed me a ninety-acre coffee farm yesterday that I liked a lot. It even comes with two dogs." Sam said. The look of surprise on Jessica's face was priceless.

"It comes with dogs?" She asked.

"Yeah, the owners haven't been home in six years, and they want to leave the dogs with the only place they know as home. The dogs think the caretakers are their masters since the owners haven't been back. No need to rock the boat, I guess, if I buy the place. Besides, I like dogs. Speaking of boats, I'm thinking about starting an interisland ferry," said Sam.

"You know you'd have a better chance of going to Mars first, right?" Jessica said.

Sam turned his head from the golf cart path and looked at Jessica for a moment, a gleam in his eye. "Yeah, I know. I like a challenge, what can I say?"

Jessica could see why Sam was so wealthy. He had big ideas, and he went after what he wanted. She didn't want to discourage him, but she thought she should warn him.

"I think the ferry is a good idea. But you'll have a fight on your hands with the people on Maui and Kauai. Hire good lawyers. You'll need them."

Everything seemed to roll off Sam's back. He laughed. "Somehow I don't doubt you for a minute."

❀

GOVERNOR FITCH WAS a short heavyset man with a beard and a bad toupee. He was at the Ming to golf with Mr. Lau and discuss when the gambling laws in Hawaii would change. Fitch wanted to legalize gambling, and Mr. Lau had put close to a million dollars into Fitch's reelection campaign through various phony shell companies. The way Mr. Lau saw it, he owned the governor, and he wanted the law changed yesterday.

Sam and Jessica arrived at the Hibiscus Room at the Ming at 9 a.m. to meet Governor Fitch. Mr. Lau hadn't planned to stick around—that was, until he saw Jessica was with Sam. Then he made it a point to stay.

Governor Fitch and Sam stepped off to the side of the room to have their meeting. Mr. Lau asked Jessica if he could show her something while the two men were talking. She agreed, and they stepped into the room next door, where there was a mockup of a proposed extension to the Ming. It showed the Ming as one big resort, with the grounds of the model extended to include the Aloha Village.

After looking at the model for a minute and noticing a proposed golf course where her father's bungalow sat, Jessica had to fight to keep her composure. She shoved her feelings aside and went into murder cop mode. With no emotion on her face, she remarked, "I notice your model encompasses our resort."

Mr. Lau smiled. "This would be the plan, if we could come to an agreeable price for Aloha Village at a later date. I don't expect you to make any major decisions right now, at this time of great sorrow in your life," he said solemnly.

Sure, you don't, you son of a bitch. With a half smile on her face, she turned to go back to the Hibiscus Room and see if Sam's meeting with Governor Fitch was over.

Fitch and Sam were just finishing up. They shook hands, and Sam said, "Thank you so much for your help today."

The governor smiled. "It was a pleasure doing business with you, Mr. Stewart."

Sam and Jessica got back in the golf cart and returned to Aloha Village. Jessica was silent. Since the governor was on board with Sam's plan to start a ferry, Sam was all smiles. Except for the fact that it would require a significant campaign contribution to the governor's reelection fund. Sam hated paying politicians to get them to do their jobs, but he looked at it as a necessary evil.

"So what did you and Mr. Lau do in the room next door?" Sam asked Jessica.

She told him about his plans to build a golf course where her father's bungalow sat, and Sam noted her clenched jaw.

As a homicide detective, nothing bothered her at work except dead kids. But this was different. This was her family, and she was having a hard time suppressing her emotions. Her father had fought the mainland developers for years to keep Kona from becoming like Honolulu. Jessica understood her father's love of Aloha Village and the people who came to work and play there. And for some Chinese gangster to come in and build a golf course on top of what her father held sacred, that was just unbearable for Jessica.

"Why do you want to start a ferry system?" Jessica asked, changing the subject. "Wouldn't a cruise line or something be more profitable?"

It didn't take Sam more than a second to respond, "After the first billion, making money gets boring, and you look for ways to help your fellow man instead. Well, at least some of us do when we get to that income level. And besides, I already own a cruise line."

Jessica didn't care for rich men. All the perks that came with them were nice, but there was a lot of baggage that went along with that. In high school, she had worked part-time jobs at various resorts on the Kona coast and had been hit on by a lot of wealthy men. Most of them were married dirtbags looking for something on the side. That didn't seem to be the case with Sam.

Unlike the others she had known over the years, Sam appeared to be the real deal. A good guy with a good heart. She was growing rather fond of him, even though the circumstances of their being together right now were not what she would consider ideal.

❀

AFTER JESSICA AND SAM LEFT, the governor and Mr. Lau sat at the private bar inside the Ming.

"Well, did you make her an offer?" the governor asked Mr. Lau.

"No, but I let her know an offer was on the table at a later date if she would like to sell."

Governor Fitch narrowed his eyes and puffed out his chest. "If she doesn't accept the offer, let me know. I'll figure out a way to impose eminent domain so you can take possession of Aloha Village and build the casino once gambling is legal." He raised his whiskey glass in a toast. "No worries, my friend. We will get control of that property."

Oh yes, the governor and Mr. Lau were partners in crime. Governor Fitch would do everything he could to get gambling legalized in Hawaii so he and Mr. Lau would have the largest casino in the state. And if Fitch got reelected, they would have the only casino in the state of Hawaii. He would make sure any competitor thinking about opening a casino would face years of government red tape.

But they needed the Aloha Village property to achieve their goal. They had to have it. What Governor Fitch didn't know was that Mr. Lau would kill if he had to to get what he wanted.

7

PUA CANCER

J essica sat on the lanai of her dad's bungalow, staring at the ocean. Comet's head lay on her lap, and she rubbed his ears while listening to the surf crash on the beach. The house phone rang and jolted her out of her trance. She couldn't believe her dad still had a landline.

Pushing Comet off her lap, Jessica went into the kitchen and grabbed the phone off the counter. She glanced at the caller ID and saw it was Pua. She felt a twinge of guilt in her gut. She had paid no attention to Pua since she had gotten back to Kona. "Hey, sis. How are you feeling these days?" Jessica asked quietly.

"Like I've been beat with a stick. I suspect in a hundred years from now, people will look back at how we treated cancer patients and think how barbaric it was," Pua answered.

"I'm so sorry, honey. I know I haven't been there for you. That changes today," Jessica said, slapping herself on the forehead.

"No worries, Jess. I know you've been busy trying to figure out what happened to Dad."

Jessica appreciated her sister's understanding but felt guilty just the same.

"I thought I'd give you a heads-up. Uncle Jin's coming over to visit. He heard you were back and called to say he wants to talk story. He didn't elaborate," Pua said.

Jessica went from guilty to annoyed. "I see he still has eyes in Kona," she mused. "I don't want him on the property. Hell, I don't even want to be out in public with him. Tell him we'll meet at your place, if that's okay with you," Jessica said as she tapped her fingers on the counter.

"Sure, we can meet here at my place. Uncle likes coming here anyway. He's been a good uncle to Kainoa the last few years. I hope you guys can set aside your differences."

Jessica frowned but held her tongue and decided to change the subject. "Do you have plans today? Can we hang out?"

"Who are you, and what have you done with my sister, Jessica?" Pua asked. Both of the sisters laughed. "I have plans to show your boyfriend Sam a property today," she teased.

"Sam is not my boyfriend," Jessica answered.

"Okay, if you say so. But I've seen how you look at him." Pua seemed to take pleasure in teasing Jessica. "You're welcome to tag along. I'm sure he won't mind. Besides, maybe you'll want to go into real estate now that you've retired from the force."

Jessica knew Pua was trying to be nice, but the thought of selling real estate was the last thing on her mind. "Okay, it's a deal," Jessica said and hung up the phone.

Pua called Sam and asked if he minded Jessica tagging along for the day when they went to view property. Sam was almost giddy with excitement at the chance to spend the day with her. He had two places he wanted to look at. One was up mauka. It was a coffee farm. The other was right on the ocean at Keauhou Bay. He liked them both but decided he would let Jessica pick which one he bought, though he wouldn't tell her she had the deciding vote. If things went the way he wanted, she would live there someday.

❦

Mike Murphy's bungalow sat on a hill overlooking the entire Aloha Village Resort and the ocean, so Jessica could see Sam as he walked up the long driveway. "Aloha, Sam," she said as he neared the lanai.

"Aloha, good morning. It's a beautiful day in Hawaii," Sam answered.

Jessica stood up and walked down the three steps of the lanai to give Sam a hug. After the warm embrace, she handed him a small gift box she had been waiting to give him.

"What's this?" Sam shook the box.

"Just a little something for your generosity. Open it."

Sam untied the bow and opened the box. Inside was an exquisite hand-carved fish hook necklace made of koa wood and tipped with cow bone. "It was my father's. He would have wanted you to have it, and I want you to have it too."

"I'm honored, thank you." Sam slipped the necklace over his head. Jessica reached over and turned the hook to point towards Sam's heart. "There, that's better. That's how it's supposed to be."

Sam reached into the pocket of his aloha shirt and pulled out a yellow plumeria flower. He placed it above her right ear and went to kiss her on the cheek, but instead Jessica turned her mouth towards Sam's. Their lips met and opened to the swirling of their tongues meeting for the first time. At that moment, Jessica knew they were meant to be together; she couldn't fight it any longer.

After a few minutes of exploring each other's tongues, they sat on the lanai swing side by side and took turns rubbing Comet's ears. Sam and Jessica rocked back and forth in total bliss while they waited for Pua to show up.

When Pua arrived and saw Sam and Jessica sitting on the swing together, there was no doubt in her mind that something was going on between the two of them. Jessica had a glow to her face that Pua had not seen in years. She felt happy inside that her sister had found a good man after the nightmare divorce she had gone through two years prior.

SAM AND JESSICA stood on the lanai and leaned on the rail, taking in the magnificent view of Keauhou Bay. They watched the warm tropical ocean lap at the shoreline, with yellow tangs swimming by the front of the estate.

"Which place do you like better?" Sam asked. "Up mauka was nice. The view of the entire Kona coast was spectacular. But the view here is also spectacular, and you can be in the water in seconds, just like at Aloha Village."

Jessica's face lit up as she pointed towards a low-flying pueo over the bay. "There's your answer, Sam. The owl is sacred in Hawaiian culture. It's an omen."

It was apparent Jessica liked the place on the water better, and Sam decided right then that he would make an offer. Now if he could just get over that fear of sharks, he might consider swimming in the bay.

Pua walked up and interrupted their moment of bliss. "What do you think Sam?" Pua asked.

"Make a full-price offer," answered Sam.

Pua frowned.

"The seller's agent just told me that there'd been an offer made while we were here."

Sam didn't bat an eye. "Tell the sellers agent that whatever the offer from the other side, we'll top it by one hundred thousand dollars."

"I'm told the seller accepted the offer."

Sam didn't like being told he couldn't have something.

"Tell the seller's agent that I'll pay the buyer a hundred thousand to walk away, and I'll give the seller a hundred thousand more than the offer they accepted."

"I'll make the offer," Pua said.

UNCLE JIN TANAKA was the boss of the yakuza in Hawaii. He was a major reason Jessica had moved to the mainland twenty-one years ago to continue her career in law enforcement. It would've been impossible to remain on the job in Kona. The police suspected Uncle Jin was responsible for a majority of the organized crime in the Hawaiian Islands. She knew a lot of cops who looked the other way when it came to the yakuza and family, but she would not be one of them. She didn't like the thought of being under constant scrutiny, with half of her family being Japanese gang members—or the prospect of having to arrest one of them someday.

It was quite the family tree. On her father's side, federal agents and cops, and on her mother's side, Japanese gangsters. It always made for interesting conversation at the Thanksgiving table.

Both federal and state law enforcement agencies suspected Jin Tanaka of ordering half a dozen murders in Hawaii over a thirty-year period. But he was known for supporting various local charities and was a pillar of the community on both Oahu and the big island, according to local civic leaders—at least, the ones he wasn't trying to extort money from. Half the people who knew him thought he was a saint, and the other half thought he was the devil himself.

The FBI had tried for years to get enough evidence against Jin Tanaka to go to trial, but they could never infiltrate the yakuza. And since the murders were of some of Oahu's most unsavory characters, the cops had done the minimum amount of investigation and called it a day so they could move on to more pressing issues, like seat belt enforcement.

Pua picked up Uncle Jin at the airport just as she had every other Saturday for the last couple years and brought him to her house, where Jessica was waiting. Kainoa loved his uncle and looked forward to his frequent visits, especially since his dad had long since abandoned him. He would take Kainoa to the beach, and they would play in the surf for hours and then get shave ice.

Kainoa was excited as always to see Uncle Jin and ran up and gave him a great big hug when he walked in the door with Pua. "Go beach, Uncle?" he asked with a big smile on his face.

"Soon. I have to talk to your Auntie Jessica first."

Pua grabbed Kainoa's hand and led him back to his bedroom. She didn't know what Uncle wanted to talk with Jessica about, and she didn't want to know.

Jessica was sitting at the kitchen table, sipping coffee. Uncle Jin filled a coffee cup of his own and sat down across from her.

They stared at each other for a moment before Jessica asked, "So what do you want to talk about?"

Uncle Jin smiled. "That's what I love about you, kid. You get right to the point. So I'll do the same. You have a problem," he said gruffly.

"Yeah, I know—you for a relative," Jessica snapped back.

Uncle Jin ignored her comment. "The governor and the Triads are planning to take control of Aloha Village."

"How?" Jessica asked.

"My source tells me Governor Fitch is looking into taking the resort by eminent domain if you turn down Mr. Lau's next offer."

Jessica took a sip of her coffee and then asked, "Why are you telling me this, and why do you care?"

"Because the Triads are trying to take over Hawaii, and we can't let that happen."

"We?"

"Like it or not, we must work together to fight the Triads and the governor. I've heard rumblings that the Chinese government is behind them and may have plans for Hawaii."

Jessica pulled a piece of nicotine gum out of her purse and bit down on it. "Me, work with you, the yakuza? Remember the last time that happened? You went to prison. And do I need to remind you that my father's side of the family puts your side of the family in jail for a career?"

Uncle Tanaka smiled. "I know that. I also know you held back in court. Or else I'd still be in prison."

"Let's just say my father is what kept you from getting a life sentence. And he's not here to protect you the next time, if there is one."

"If the Triads and the governor get their way, Kona as we know it will cease to exist. There only needs to be one Waikiki in Hawaii."

Uncle Jin took the final sip of his coffee and got up from the table and walked over to the sink to rinse the cup.

Jessica spat her gum out. "As much as I'd like to save Hawaii from the Triads and the governor, I don't have time. I'm more interested in finding out who killed my father."

Uncle Jin looked out the window over the kitchen sink at the ocean. "I'm almost sure Mr. Lau gave the order to sabotage your father's airplane."

Jessica changed her demeanor from annoyed to all business and asked him, "How do you know? Do you have any evidence?"

"One of my people works at the airport and saw someone coming out of your father's hangar the night before he crashed his plane. It was Woo Ching."

Jessica said nothing. She sat there and stared at her uncle and wondered how much of what he said was true. What was in it for him? There was no love lost between him and her father. Jessica doubted he cared one way or the other about her father's death. As far as Uncle Jin was concerned, it was one less Murphy in the world he had to contend with.

Mike Murphy and Uncle Jin hadn't been enemies—Mike was the only Murphy who hadn't been in law enforcement. But just the same, they hadn't been fans of each other. It was Uncle Jack that Uncle Jin hated. He was the one responsible for sending Jin to prison. Unlike Jessica, Uncle Jack had done his best to lock up Uncle Jin for as long as possible. Now that Uncle Jack was living in Kona, Uncle Jin pretty much kept a low profile when he came to the big island and saved all his nefarious activities for Oahu. Uncle Jin only came to Kona to play with Kainoa and check on his feisty ninety-three-year-old mother, who still worked in the family coffee farm in Holualoa. Grandma Tanaka had never forgiven Jessica for testifying against Uncle Jin in court, and they hadn't spoken to each other since that day years ago. Pua and Jasmine still kept in contact with Uncle Jin, but they weren't close to Grandma Tanaka.

Helen Tanaka wasn't the grandmotherly type. Or the motherly type for that matter. Evil and vindictive were her two best qualities if you asked Jessica. Which she was sure had something to do with her three sons all becoming high-ranking members of the yakuza.

The thing about Uncle Jin was that he had respect for the old Hawaii that Mike Murphy had fought hard to protect from mainland developers and Mr. Lau. Uncle Jin also wanted to keep Aloha Village from falling into their hands. Plus he was no fan of Governor Fitch, who he had also been paying off for years to leave the yakuza alone on Oahu. If Uncle Jin could get Mr. Lau put away for Mike Murphy's murder, that would be one less competitor in the crime world of Hawaii. And if he could get Jessica to do all the work, that would be even better.

Pua and Kainoa came back into the living room in their swimsuits. Jessica and Pua were going scuba diving in Puako, and Kainoa and Uncle Jin were going to the beach.

"Which beach are you guys going to?" Pua asked.

"The Ming," Uncle answered.

"Their beach sucks. Why are you going there?" Pua asked.

Jessica interjected, "He's going over there to pee on their tree." Pua looked perplexed. "I'll explain on the way to Puako," Jessica said.

Uncle Jin said nothing but had a slight grin on his face as he grabbed Kainoa's hand to leave.

8

PUAKO

"We'll stop at the dive shop and pick up two tanks and then head up to Puako, if that sounds good to you, Jess."

It was a gorgeous morning, with Hawaiian slack key guitar music filling the cab of Pua's custom Toyota Tacoma. The sisters cruised north on the Queen K Highway, as the locals liked to call it.

After about twenty miles, Jessica asked Pua, "What happened to all the coral graffiti on the lava flows?"

"Some group of self-appointed do-gooders with a lot of time on their hands deemed it an eyesore and removed the coral. Now people just use spray paint to write on the lava. I don't know why people can't just live and let live."

"Look, it's so clear you can see Maui," said, Jessica, pointing at Mount Haleakala in the distance.

"Yeah, the volcano has mellowed out the last couple of years, and we have a lot more clear days now," said Pua.

After a nice drive along the Kona coast to Puako, the sisters put on their wetsuits and scuba tanks and did a quick safety check of their gear. Then they discussed their dive plan before snorkeling out to the drop-down spot.

Since the ocean surface looked more like a lake that day, almost flat, underwater visibility was excellent at about eighty feet. After dropping down about thirty feet below the ocean's surface and swimming along the reef, Jessica felt her body relax for the first time in a long while. *Ah, zero gravity is a beautiful thing,* Jessica thought. It felt so good to get back in the ocean again.

The reef looked healthy, with lots of tropical fish and a sea turtle here and there.

A few feet away, Pua was playing with an octopus she had found that was trying to blend in next to a coral head. She handed it to Jessica so she could feel its soft, velvety skin.

About that time, a dolphin swam up from out of the deep and went right up to Jessica. The poor creature had fishing line wrapped around it that cut into its fluke and needed help to remove the tangled mess.

Jessica and Pua both worked at a quick pace to untangle and cut free the fishing line that was torturing the poor creature. It was unbelievable how patient the dolphin was, rolling over right in front of them so they could cut away the tangled mess.

After they freed the dolphin from the fishing line, it gave them both what appeared to be a smile and swam off into the abyss, gone just as fast as it had appeared.

Pua and Jessica stared at each other for a minute in total disbelief. It was a moment they knew they would never forget, and they savored every minute as they swam along the reef, thinking about what had just happened.

Jessica looked at her air pressure gauge and signaled Pua she was low on air. She pointed up towards the surface, and Pua signaled back okay.

As soon as the sisters broke the surface, it became obvious they were in big trouble. While they had been down below, a freak storm had blown in. The ocean surface had gone from calm to large swells in less than an hour. With six-to-eight-foot waves pounding the shoreline, getting back to the beach would be dangerous.

Jessica pulled the regulator out of her mouth and yelled at Pua over the sound of the wind, "I don't know about you, Pua, but getting pounded into the reef wasn't in my game plan today."

Pua had surfed on the women's pro tour in her late teens and early twenties and could make it through the big surf. Jessica always stayed on the beach when the surf was over five feet. This surf was far bigger than any she had ever body-surfed, and swimming through it with dive gear on was the last thing she wanted to do.

Pua dropped her weight belt and took off her BCD. Then she unstrapped the scuba tank and let it drop to the bottom before putting the BCD back on to use as a life jacket. "You have to drop your tank," she yelled at Jessica.

Shit, Jessica thought, *we're really going to do this*. She followed Pua's instructions and dropped her gear in forty feet of water, watching it sink to the bottom.

"No turning back now, Jess. Let's go."

The good news was that at least they had fins on. The bad news was an even bigger set of waves rolled in, twelve to fifteen feet in height.

"Let's try to body-surf in," Pua yelled. Jessica nodded in agreement as the next big wave came rolling in. They both put their heads down and swam as fast as they could to catch the wave.

Pua was a much stronger swimmer than Jessica and caught the wave and rode it all the way to the beach. As she crawled up to the beach, Pua looked back to see where Jessica was. When she didn't see her, she threw off her BCD and ran back into the surf to find her sister.

Jessica swam just slowly enough that she hadn't caught the fifteen-foot rogue wave but had gone over the falls, as the surfers called it. Because she'd been late in catching the wave, she'd been at the top of it when it had crashed onto the shallow reef and knocked her out.

Between waves, Pua found Jessica floating facedown close to shore. She grabbed one of the straps of Jessica's BCD and flipped her over, swimming as fast as she could with one arm. She kicked her fins harder than she ever had in her life. If she didn't, they would get pounded on the reef by the next wave, and that would be the end of them.

Pua dragged Jessica's head and chest out of the water and onto the beach just enough so she could start CPR. Jessica's lips were blue, and every minute counted.

"You're not dying today, bitch!" Pua yelled at Jessica as she pumped her chest.

Thirty pumps and two breaths were all Pua could remember to do for CPR. It was just going to have to work, because Pua's energy was fading fast and she was ready to collapse.

About two hundred and fifty yards down the beach a nurse who was taking photos happened to see what was going on. She ran up to help and took over the CPR.

"It's okay, honey. I called 911 as soon I saw what was going on," said the nurse.

Sam had planned on meeting Pua and Jessica after their dive so they could all go to Cafe Pesto for lunch. When they weren't at the boat ramp at the agreed-upon time, he scouted around the area for them. Fifteen minutes later, he found Pua's Tacoma parked on a side road near the beach, and he stopped to see if they were nearby.

Sam rounded the corner from the road to the beach and saw Pua and the nurse huddled over Jessica about a hundred feet down the beach. He knew it wasn't good and ran to where they were.

"What happened? Where're the paramedics? How can I help?" Sam fired the questions at Pua.

"Call 911 and find out where the hell the paramedics are," the nurse barked as she pumped Jessica's chest.

Sam pulled out his phone and called 911. The operator said the paramedics were on the way, but some kind of equipment issue was slowing them down.

"What about the fire department helicopter?" Sam asked.

"It's out of service for repairs," the operator answered. Annoyed did not begin to describe the look on Sam's face.

Sam called Uncle Jack. Ten minutes later, a Black Hawk helicopter landed in a clearing near the beach and flew Jessica to the Kona hospital.

SIX HOURS LATER, Sam, Pua, Uncle Jack and Jasmine sat in the waiting area at the Kona hospital. Nobody said a word until Dr. Kiyoshi came into the room. Then they all jumped to their feet, sounding like a group of reporters as they fired off one question after the other. "How is she? Is she going to be okay?"

Dr. Kiyoshi smiled. "She'll be fine. She's awake now. We want to run more tests and keep her overnight. You guys should go home and come back in the morning to pick her up."

Everyone shook Dr. Kiyoshi's hand and broke down into tears and hugs. Even Uncle Jack showed signs of his eyes misting over.

Pua had to get home because of Kainoa. Jasmine had to get back to running the resort. Uncle Jack had to go explain why he'd used a marijuana eradication helicopter to save a civilian. And Sam had resolved to stay in the waiting room until Jessica was ready to go home the next morning.

In the morning, a nurse came and woke Sam, who was sleeping in a chair. "You're waiting for Jessica Kealoha?"

Sam nodded.

"We'll bring her out in a few minutes and you can take her home."

Sam stood up, stretched, yawned and waited until Jessica came through the double doors in a wheelchair. Jessica had hoped it was Sam waiting for her, and she couldn't be happier to see his smiling face. Though he looked like he had been through the ringer after sleeping in the waiting room all night. Five-o'clock shadow, bloodshot eyes, messed-up hair. Not your typical billionaire look. And Jessica loved all of it.

Sam wanted to hug Jessica, but she put her hand up to stop him. "There's nothing I would love more than a hug from you. But I have two broken ribs from all the fun I had yesterday."

Sam recoiled as if from a hot flame. "I'm so sorry, honey." He then reached down and caressed her hand and kissed it. "I almost lost you. Never do that again. Okay?" His eyes were glazed over.

As Sam and Jessica drove along Mamalahoa Highway, Jessica didn't take the view for granted. The plumeria flowers along the highway were more beautiful that morning than they had ever been before, the ocean bluer and the salt in the air more soothing. Nothing like being dead yesterday to make one grateful to be alive today. And for Sam, almost losing Jessica made him even more determined to enjoy every minute with her from that day forward.

"Pua is working on getting the house at Keauhou Bay. I wish it were ours now. I mean, ready to move in. I'd just take you there." Jessica looked at Sam for a second with admiration and then looked back towards the road as they drove through Kainaliu towards Kailua Town.

Jessica reached over and rested her hand on Sam's thigh. "If you don't mind, I'd like to stop at the old airport."

"Sure," said Sam. Jessica sighed. It was nice to be taken care of for once.

"I'd just like to sit on a picnic table underneath one of the kiawe trees and watch the surf for a little while before going home."

And that was what they did. They sat like two bumps on a log for an hour, staring at the ocean. Watching the surfers catch waves, then get barrel rolled and glide all the way to the beach as if on a magic carpet.

Jessica thought about what had happened the day before, how the sea had taken its best shot at her and had come up short. But she knew she had been fortunate. Jessica didn't view it as any god looking out for her. Getting slammed onto the reef was bad luck. Wrong place at the wrong time. It was as simple as that. Or at least that was her first thought, since she had decided a long time ago that there was no God. And if there was, he didn't seem to care about people, as evidenced by all the rotten things that happened in the world.

Sam said it was obvious someone or something was looking out for her. The nurse who'd been on the beach, in the right place at the right time. Uncle Jack having access to a helicopter by making a phone call. The most senior ER doctor being on duty at the Kona hospital when she arrived. Sam didn't believe in coincidences. He believed everything happened for a reason. They were opposites when it came to their view on whether or not there was someone or something behind the scenes overseeing things. Jessica had never wavered in her beliefs before, but she was reconsidering.

As they sat mesmerized at the picnic table, watching the surfers rip up and down the waves and the fishing boats cruise by, Jessica said, "Yesterday when I was on that beach and not breathing, I had an out-of-body experience. And the funny thing about it? It was okay if that was how it would end. But the paradox was, I wasn't ready to leave yet. It must have been my sense of making things right pulling me back.

My father's murder cannot go unavenged. And if I don't bring the person responsible for his death to justice, I might as well have died."

Before Sam responded, an HC 130 Coast Guard plane flew overhead. The only time you saw them in Kona was when someone was having a bad day. And for the first time in years, Jessica said a short silent prayer for whoever the Coast Guard was looking for. Just in case it turned out it mattered.

🏵️

SAM TOOK Jessica back to her dad's bungalow, where everyone was out front on the lanai, waiting for her. There must have been fifty people there to greet Jessica. It looked like a gathering at the courthouse. Most of them were cops, and two were Jessica's yakuza uncles. Jessica looked at Sam as they drove up the driveway and saw the crowd waiting out front.

"Know anything about this?"

Sam shook his head no.

Only in Hawaii was what came to mind when Jessica recognized all the people she knew there from both sides of the fence as far as the law was concerned.

Sam parked the truck and announced to the crowd, "No hugs, she has two broken ribs." And then he opened her door and slowly helped her out of the truck up the steps of the lanai to an empty chair.

For the next hour, Jessica's family and friends showered her with love, letting her know how glad they were that she was still with them and hadn't been taken by the sea.

After everyone left, including Sam, Jessica went inside. There was a message on the answering machine from Mr. Jennings's law office. It said that said Mr. Lau had made another offer to buy Aloha Village, this time for full retail. Even with all the work the property still needed to have done.

Jessica called Mr. Jennings back and told him Mr. Lau couldn't buy Aloha Village at any price.

Jessica didn't care how much money he offered. Just like her father, she would never sell it to him. Especially now that she knew Woo Ching had been spotted at the airport, coming out of the hangar Mike kept his plane in, and was suspected of causing her father's death.

9

STAGE FOUR

J essica called Pua the next morning to set a lunch date for later that day at Kona Inn. It was Kona's oldest watering hole and a favorite of Jessica's since she was a little girl. The old fans hanging from the ceiling and the koa wood canoe over the bar were remnants of days gone by in Kona.

Jessica realized after her near-death experience that it was time to put the living first. While it was important to bring her father's killer to justice, spending time with Pua now was more important since she didn't know if Pua would survive cancer.

When Jessica and Pua arrived at the Kona Inn later that day, "Over the Rainbow" by Brother Iz played at a low volume in the background, and Jessica felt a sense of well-being she only felt when she was in Hawaii.

The two sisters sat at a table next to the three-foot-high rock wall closest to the ocean. It had a clear view of Kailua Bay and the tour boats as they came and went from the Kailua Pier. A few minutes later, the middle-aged waitress approached their table. She was tanned and had a friendly smile and a beautiful plumeria flower above her left ear.

"Aloha. Would you ladies like something to drink?"

"I'll have iced tea," said Jessica.

"I'll have the same," answered Pua.

After the waitress walked away, Pua asked Jessica. "Are you still on the wagon?"

"Yeah, something like that."

"How long has it been this time?"

"In dog years?" Jessica smiled, then her expression turned serious. "Three years, two months and six days. But who's counting?"

"Way to go, sis."

"Thanks."

As they sat on the lanai and sipped their iced teas, they took in the view of the palm trees and turquoise bay with small white-water waves breaking at the shoreline fronting Kona Inn. They watched two young local kids play in the surf at the small beach across the bay next to the pier, just like they had when they were kids. The trade winds were blowing, and that kept the humidity to a pleasant level. It was almost a perfect day.

Jessica didn't want to ask, but she had to know. "Did you get the PET scan results this morning?"

The grim look on Pua's face gave Jessica her answer. "It's not good. The cancer has spread to my liver." Pua had been keeping it together up until this point, but now her eyes filled with tears.

Unlike when Pua had told Jessica about her cancer at the Marlin House, Jessica decided she would not cry. She had to be strong for Pua.

"Take it one day at a time. It'll be okay."

Pua dabbed her eyes with her napkin. "The doctor says he wants to take out part of the liver." Jessica scooted her chair over next to Pua and put her arm around her sister's shoulder. For a few minutes, they didn't say a word, just watched the canoes paddling in Kailua Bay, getting ready for the weekend races. The silence was broken when Jessica's phone buzzed in her purse. She glanced down and saw it was Mr. Jennings's number and decided she better take it. "Hello, this is Jessica."

"Hi, Jessica. I got your message declining Mr. Lau's offer. I wish you would reconsider. Finding another buyer willing to pay full price for Aloha Village in its current condition will be hard, if not impossible."

"The answer is still no, Mr. Jennings." Jessica hung up the phone and continued to rub Pua's shoulder, which she had been squeezing the hell out of while talking on the phone.

"What was that all about?" asked Pua.

"Mr. Lau made a full-price offer on Aloha Village. And I told Mr. Jennings to tell Lau that Aloha Village is not for sale."

Pua went from solemn to irritated. "You didn't plan on running that by Jasmine and me?"

"Do you want to sell to the man who's most likely responsible for Dad's death and would turn the Village into a casino?" Jessica countered.

"If you weren't here, I'd sell Aloha Village right now and be rid of that nightmare. It's a never-ending money pit, and the sooner we're out from under it, the better."

The conversations of other diners sitting on the patio came to an abrupt halt. Everyone heard Pua's angry response and stared at her and Jessica.

Jessica didn't react; she didn't want to get into an argument in public about Aloha Village because she knew it would get back to Mr. Lau and the less he knew about the Murphy ohana, the better.

"I'm just trying to do the right thing here," Jessica said quietly.

Pua shook her head. She knew Jessica was right. She was

just upset that Jessica hadn't at least mentioned it to her and Jasmine first.

"Have you considered asking Sam if he'd be interested in buying or investing in the resort? Or what about Uncle Jack? Dad alluded more than once to Uncle having made a lot of money investing in stocks."

Jessica hadn't thought about Uncle Jack. The only thing she knew for sure was she would not ask Sam for the money to save Aloha Village since nothing made couples fight more than money and relatives. Then she thought, We're a couple?

Jessica wasn't optimistic by nature. She believed that what could go wrong would go wrong most of the time. She knew this wasn't a healthy way to think, and she fought it on a daily basis. But this time, she knew in her heart everything would be okay, all of it. Pua, Aloha Village and her relationship with Sam. Nothing like a near-death experience to get your attitude about life straightened out, she thought.

"We need to form a hui to buy the resort," Jessica said with excitement in her voice. "What do you think?"

Pua was chewing on a cold French fry and thought about what Jessica had said for a minute before answering. "Maybe we could get Uncle Jack to invest."

Pua and Jessica were so excited they drove out to the harbor to see if Uncle Jack was in port, since he wasn't answering his phone as usual. They couldn't wait to pitch him their idea to save the Village.

Erica Black, a local real estate broker who was sitting two tables away and heard Pua's outburst earlier, called Mr. Lau as soon as she got back to her office.

UNCLE JACK WAS SITTING in the fighting chair on the deck of the Hui Hou, reading the local fishing news and puffing on a cigar, when Pua and Jessica drove up. So much for peace and quiet, he thought when he saw Pua's truck parked in front of the Hui Hou's slip.

"Hey, Uncle," Pua and Jessica called out as they walked down the dock towards the boat. Uncle Jack didn't know what to think. He couldn't remember the last time he'd seen those two together and happy about it.

"For someone who was dead a couple days ago, you look pretty good, Jess," said Uncle Jack.

"Let's say I'm reenergized," said Jessica.

Pua never minced words or wasted time when money was involved. She told Uncle Jack what they had in mind about forming a hui of investors to save Aloha Village. Since real estate was her thing, Jessica kept her mouth shut and let Pua do all the talking, nodding at the appropriate times.

"I think it's a great idea. But I'm broke. You know the old cliché—'if you want to be a millionaire in Hawaii, bring two million with you.' A month ago, I paid off the Hui Hou and its slip because I didn't want any payments when I retire for good."

Pua and Jessica both looked like they'd had their balloons popped.

"But, I think I know where you can get the money. If I were you, I'd call an employee meeting at the Village and pitch them the idea of making all the employees part owners." Uncle Jack said.

"Dad paid them well, but I don't think he paid them that kind of money," Pua said. The optimism in Jessica's face had disappeared.

"You're right. But two ladies that teach lei making to the guests are from a family that owned half of Honolulu until a few years ago. When they cashed out during the last real estate boom, each family member walked away with about three million dollars each. They don't work in the Village because they have to. They do it to share the aloha of old Hawaii with the visitors."

🐚

ALL TWENTY-THREE ALOHA Village employees gathered Saturday morning at the beach for the meeting. Most of them had worked at the resort for over twenty years, and it was more like a working ohana than what most people would consider a job.

Jessica started the meeting by thanking everyone for their years of service and then got right to the heart of the matter.

"Aloha Village is broke. We can't borrow enough money to fend off foreclosure. The owner of the Ming next door wants to buy us and expand the Ming to include a casino damn near on top of where we're standing."

Auntie Loana had worked in the Village since the early seventies. She stood up and said, "No can!" with a thick pidgin accent.

Jessica nodded in agreement. "We won't sell the Village to them at any price. But we have a problem. We need to sell to someone, and the Village isn't in sellable condition right now. We want to form a hui to fund the resort going forward and would like to offer you guys the opportunity to be in charge of your destiny."

Auntie Loana stood back up. "How much you need, sista?"

Jessica looked Auntie in the eye. "We need at least five hundred thousand to buy us some time. Or a little over a million to fix the Village and get the trust landowner to renew the lease for another twenty years."

"Only a million? Shoots. Can handle." And Auntie Loana sat back down.

Jessica couldn't believe what she had just heard. Nobody knew Auntie Loana had that kind of money. She had been driving the same Kona cruiser to work for the last ten years. It was an old faded red '83 Toyota Tercel. Other than one gold bracelet that said "Kuipo," she didn't look like she had two nickels to rub together from all outward appearances.

"Okay, we all work for Auntie now," said Jessica, and everyone laughed. And one by one, everyone hugged Auntie Loana.

After the meeting, Auntie Loana got her checkbook and wrote a check for one point two million dollars. She'd included a couple hundred thousand extra, just in case the resort needed it. As she handed Jessica the check, she said, "This is a loan. I don't want to own the Village. You pay me back when you can." Jessica and Pua both had tears of gratitude in their eyes.

"Wait until Monday to deposit. I got to move the funds from my investment account on the mainland to the local bank." Jessica and Pua looked at each other in amazement. They'd never dreamed Auntie Loana was this sophisticated secret millionaire.

"Okay, Auntie. Monday," Jessica answered.

AFTER THE PHONE call from Erica Black, Mr. Lau decided that Jessica must die if he was going to be able to buy Aloha Village since it was clear she was just as stubborn as her father had been and would never sell the property to him.

With Jessica out of the way, Lau was confident that Pua would sell Aloha Village.

Lau had had a spy working at Aloha Village for the last year who had instructions to report anything that would help the Triads take control of the Village.

When Lau got wind of the beach meeting, he called Woo Ching into his office at the Ming. "I need you to take care of a problem for me." Lau proceeded to tell Woo Ching that Jessica needed to be taken out on her way to the bank

Monday morning. Woo Ching nodded and left Mr. Lau's office without a word.

Woo Ching was the Triads' most notorious hit man in Hong Kong and had been sent to the Ming in Kona for just such an occasion as this. Woo Ching's method of choice would be a car bomb. He could never plant it on Jessica's 4Runner while it was parked in the Village, though, so the next best thing was to bury the bomb alongside the road leaving the resort. Arming the bomb with a cell phone detonator, Woo Ching would wait until he saw the 4Runner leave, and then boom. End of problem.

❀

AT EIGHT THIRTY on Monday morning, Jessica sat on the lanai of her father's bungalow, having her morning tea. The trade winds had blown all the haziness out of Kona the day before, and she could see Mount Haleakala on Maui in the distance. The birds were chirping, and the surf was breaking against the shoreline—a welcome change compared to her mornings in California. When she looked out the window of her apartment in Anaheim, all she saw was a fenced-in patio with two dead plants. She couldn't keep the plants alive no matter what she did. And everywhere she looked in the city of Los Angeles, all she saw was death. She didn't miss it for a second.

As she daydreamed, a yellow plumeria flower blew onto the lanai from a nearby tree and landed near her feet. Jessica set her cup of tea down on the table and reached over to pick the flower up. She admired its beauty and then held it close to her nostrils, breathing in the sweet smell of the flower.

Her phone buzzed on the table, interrupting her early-morning serenity.

"My car has a dead battery. I need to take the 4Runner to town this morning," said Jasmine.

Jessica twirled the stem of the plumeria between her fingers. "The keys are in it. I have to go to the bank today as soon as you get back, so don't dally, okay? On second thought, never mind. I'll take Dad's Road Runner to the bank. You can keep the 4Runner all day if you need to."

"Okay, thanks, I'll come get it."

Ten minutes later, Jasmine was driving on the road that led from the Village to the highway when she noticed a herd of goats crossing the road ahead, and a stray dog following behind them as if he were part of their herd. It wasn't unusual to see goats out here, but dogs didn't venture out onto the lava flow that encased the road between Aloha Village and the main highway. Jasmine collected stray dogs like Pua collected boyfriends. When she wasn't busy working at the resort, she was volunteering at the Humane Society. She stopped the 4Runner and got out to see if she could catch the dog.

As Jasmine walked towards the stray, the dog trotted away to keep her from coming any closer. It was skittish and would not come. Jasmine and the dog were heading right towards the bomb that Woo Ching had planted alongside the road just before sunrise under the cover of darkness.

Woo Ching was nearby with binoculars and watched Jasmine and the stray head straight for the bomb. He had a perverse sense of amusement while he watched them jog towards certain death. He didn't care if he killed the wrong person.

Jasmine continued to whistle and clap her hands together, trying to entice the skittish dog to come to her. The dog must have sensed the danger looming and stopped right in its tracks a foot away from the bomb, letting her grab his collar. Woo Ching could see through his binoculars it wasn't Jessica and decided not to kill Jasmine since she wasn't the target. He knew Mr. Lau would be furious that he'd killed the wrong person.

As Woo Ching thought about blowing up Jasmine anyway, he saw a starburst-blue '69 Road Runner coming up the road from Aloha Village. Jessica was driving, with Sam Stewart sitting in the passenger seat. The grin on Woo Ching's face said it all as he looked through the binoculars.

He grasped the cell phone detonator and waited for all three of them to be in position before triggering the bomb.

10

TOO CLOSE FOR COMFORT

The thing about lava is it all looks the same. And when a lava flow is a mile-long and a mile wide, it better be marked if you want to come back to the same spot. Woo Ching had placed a small pile of white coral next to where he'd buried the bomb to mark its location so he could see it from the high ground on top of the cinder cone. What he didn't realize was there were other small piles of coral nearby. They marked a safe path to the beach for four-wheel-drive vehicles to keep them from falling into a lava tube while crossing over the flow.

Woo Ching clicked the dial button on the cell phone detonator, but the explosion he expected to kill the trio was at least a hundred feet away from them. The explosion was far enough away that Sam, Jessica, and Jasmine were out of the kill zone, and the 4Runner was positioned at such an angle that it took the brunt of the force of the blast. The front windshield was blown out, and a lava rock two feet in diameter landed on the hood.

Just before the bomb had exploded, Jasmine had run back down the road to where Sam and Jessica had stopped behind the 4Runner. She was leaning in the window, talking to them about the stray dog she had stopped for, when the bomb blast ripped through the morning calm of what looked like another perfect day in Hawaii.

"What the hell was that! Are you guys okay?" Sam said. Jasmine had been knocked down by the force of the blast. Jessica jumped out of the car to check on her.

"Are you okay, honey? Does it hurt anywhere?" Jessica could see the terror in her little sister's eyes and surveyed Jasmine for any visible shrapnel wounds, but she saw none.

"I'm okay."

Jessica scanned the surrounding area, looking for any signs of the bomber. While Sam and Jasmine were clueless, Jessica knew what had just happened. After two tours in Iraq with the National Guard, she'd see her share of IEDs in-country and knew someone had just tried to kill them.

Sam reached for his phone. "I'll call 911."

Jessica motioned to him to stop. "Don't bother. It's almost the same as calling the bad guys. I'll explain it later."

Sam was oblivious to the realities of island life. Jessica was not. She knew some of the local cops had ties to both the Triads and yakuza. Who knew? They might try to finish the botched attempt themselves.

"The first thing we need to do is get the hell off this road before something else bad happens," said Jessica. She got Jasmine and the stray border collie into the backseat of the Road Runner. Sam sat shotgun, and then they banzai'd back to the safety of Aloha Village.

When Woo Ching saw the bomb explode too far away from the targets, he heaved the cell phone detonator against a pile of rocks. He then hiked down the backside of the cinder cone to the beach and snuck back to the Ming to report the failed attempt to Mr. Lau.

❀

WOO CHING TOLD Mr. Lau the bomb had missed the target. There wasn't a trace of anger on Lau's face as he stood over the model of the proposed Ming expansion, moving pieces around the eight-foot-long table. Mr. Lau shifted his eyes towards the Triad's top assassin. "Since you failed, you must leave and go back to Hong Kong. I'll deal with this another way."

Woo Ching nodded and left the room. But Woo Ching had aspirations of being in charge of the Triads in the not-so-distant future and could not go back to Hong Kong until the job was complete. He had never failed to carry out a hit, and this would not be the first time.

❀

"GET cousin Jason and tell him to stay with you at all times until I sort this out. Under no circumstance are you to leave the Village until you hear from me." Then Jessica gave Jasmine a reassuring hug as they stood outside the resort's office.

While Jessica was getting Jasmine situated, Sam ran to his bungalow, which was a short distance from the office, to get the satellite phone he kept for emergencies. He called Jim Davis, the captain of *The Racer*.

"How far out are you? Fifteen miles? There's been an incident here, and I need you to send a security team ASAP."

"How many men, Mr. Stewart?" asked Captain Davis.

"Send ten guys via the Sikorsky and have it land on the old airstrip behind the Village. At the same time, launch the tender and send it too. I need it to take us to Honokohau Harbor. Have the team in khaki shorts and aloha shirts and tell them to keep the guns out of sight. I want them as low-profile as possible. They can use my bungalow as a command post. Continue on to Kailua Bay as planned and then set anchor there. I'll be staying there on board *The Racer* until this situation is under control."

Jim Davis had been the skipper of *The Racer* a long time and had never heard such urgency in Sam's voice. Sam hired only retired Navy SEALs to provide shipboard security and seamanship on his super yacht. Actually, "super yacht" was an understatement. *The Racer* was ninety-nine thousand tons and four hundred and fourteen feet long, with a crew of fifty-seven.

Sam walked at a brisk pace back towards the office, where Jessica had just come from. She could smell that it would rain soon and tied up her hair into a ponytail as the temperature and the humidity climbed because of the tropical storm that was approaching the big island.

"We need to get to town, but we also need not to get killed on the way there," Jessica told Sam, whispering so as not to alarm Jasmine any more than she already was, or any of the Village's guests staying who were within earshot.

Sam pulled the sat phone out of his pocket. "I have a plan. My tender will get here in about an hour, and we can take it to the Kailua Pier and get a taxi to the bank. Oh, by the way, I've taken the liberty of having some of my security force from my boat stay here and keep the Village safe."

Jessica studied Sam's face for a moment, thinking, *Who are you?* Then she said, "That would be great, thank you." In the back of her mind was, *What tender is he talking about? How big is his "boat"?*

Jessica had no choice but to let Sam help her. Self-reliant to a fault had been a thing with her, ever since her mother had passed away when she and her sisters were near adolescence. Since she was the oldest, her father had made her responsible for everything around the house.

Sam and Jessica walked down the beach towards the Ming to wait for the tender to arrive. There were a handful of guests snorkeling in the bay and one guy walking behind about twenty yards away from them with a towel and a boom box.

Jessica needed to call Uncle Jack and share the morning's assassination attempt with him, but first, she had to deal with a problem on the beach. As if the morning wasn't going badly enough, Mr. Obnoxious—as Jasmine referred to Grayson Roderick, who had checked into the resort last week and had become a thorn in Jasmine's side with his constant complaints about the resort—was now spreading his unpleasantness on the beach. One virtue of the Village, one of the selling points of Aloha Village that differentiated it from all other resorts in Hawaii, was its "unplugged" policy—no electronics in the common areas or the beach.

This guy didn't care about the rules. Jessica walked over to him and asked him politely if he could turn down the music a little. She didn't even mention that he was breaking the rules. He ignored her, talking on his cell phone. She was in no mood for this nonsense. She picked up the ghetto blaster and hurled it into the bay before walking back to where Sam was sitting on the beach.

Sam could see he would be the peacemaker here. As Mr. Obnoxious came charging over towards them, Sam jumped up and stepped in front of Jessica before the guy got within ten feet of her. Sam reached into his pocket for his wallet to offer to pay for the man's stereo. The buffoon answered with a fist coming towards Sam's face. Sam ducked and came back up with an uppercut that caught Mr. Important on the chin and knocked him right on his ass, out cold. He should've taken the money. Sam liked boxing to stay in shape almost as much as making money.

He pulled out his wallet and threw two hundred bucks at the guy. The money landed in the sand next to where Grayson Roderick had fallen. "This should cover your boom box, jerk."

When Roderick came to a few minutes later, Jasmine and cousin Jason escorted him to his bungalow so he could pack.

Oh yes, they were kicking his ass out. They'd enjoyed all of him they could stand.

"We'll refund your money. You're out of here as soon as you pack. We've called you a taxi. Or we can call the cops and have you arrested for assault. Your choice," said Jasmine. As Roderick packed, Jasmine added, "Excellent choice."

Jessica didn't even skip a beat. She had been on her phone talking to Uncle Jack's answering machine while Sam was defending her. It'd been years since a man had taken up for Jessica. A girl could get used to that. Little did Sam know, she didn't need him to defend her, but she liked that he had.

❀

Uncle Jack was in the head of the *Hui Hou* when he heard Jessica leaving a message on his machine. "Someone just tried to blow us up with an IED on the road leaving the Village."

Uncle Jack grumbled something to himself about never eating spicy Thai food again as he dialed Jessica's phone number.

"Where are you now?"

"Sitting on the beach at AVR, waiting for Sam's tender to pick us up since it's too dangerous to drive to town."

"Stop by. We need to talk."

"That's why I'm calling. I have a check to deposit that will save the Village, and I need to borrow your Bronco."

"Okay, I'll have it waiting for you. Do you have a weapon with you?"

"No, all my guns are still in the shipping container."

"I'll have a nine-millimeter ready for you too."

"Thanks." And Jessica clicked off her cell phone.

Next thing Uncle Jack did was dial Jin Tanaka.

Jin didn't recognize Uncle Jack's phone number and let it go to voicemail.

"Jin, we have a problem." Uncle Jack proceeded to leave a

message detailing what had just happened to Jessica, Sam, and Jasmine. Uncle Jack couldn't protect them, but he knew the yakuza would. They were family.

ABOUT TWENTY MINUTES before the tender arrived at Aloha Village Resort, the Sikorsky helicopter landed and dropped off the security force to secure the Village. Sam took the team leader around and introduced him to Jasmine and cousin Jason and two key employees of the small resort before going back to the beach to wait for the tender to arrive. Sam reassured Jessica that his guys would keep a low profile and would blend in so as not to alarm the guests. Jessica knew there was safety in numbers, and she felt safe with Sam. Soon, they spotted the tender coming into the bay in front of the resort. Technically, it was called a tender, but in most circles, people would call it a yacht.

"Aloha, Mr. Stewart," yelled Terry Barnes, the coxswain of Sam's tender, as he drifted the big boat up as close to the beach in front of Aloha Village as he could without getting stuck in the shallows. Sam and Jessica waded out, and Terry helped them both aboard from the rear swim deck.

"Good to see you again, Mr. Stewart," said Terry.

"As it is you, Mr. Barnes," answered Sam as he shook Terry's hand.

Sam placed his hand on the small of Jessica's back. "This is Jessica Kealoha."

"It's a pleasure to meet you, Ms. Kealoha," said Terry.

"Aloha, Terry. You can call me Jessica."

"Honey, if you go down below to the saloon, you can make yourself comfortable. I'll be down there in a minute," said Sam.

Jessica gave Sam a devilish look as she stepped thru the

glass sliding door to enter the saloon. *It's good to have someone who calls you honey*, she thought.

As Jessica headed for the saloon, Sam gave Terry instructions to take them to the *Hui Hou*'s slip at the harbor. Sam figured they could make it to the Honokohau in about twenty minutes cruising along at twenty or thirty knots, but he told Terry to cruise at five to eight knots.

"I don't care if you have to circle the green buoy at the harbor, make this about an hourlong trip to the *Hui Hou*, okay?" Said Sam.

"Aye, Captain," answered young Mr. Barnes.

As the sixty-foot tender left the bay and headed towards the open sea, Sam led Jessica by the hand from the saloon to the stateroom as if they had been there a thousand times before.

"We almost died today. And we may die tomorrow. We don't know. But I know one thing."

Jessica raised her hand to Sam's lips and touched them with a single finger, whispering, "Shh."

Sam hugged Jessica pulling her tight against him, and then he kissed her on the neck right behind her right ear and worked his way down towards her shoulder. She tingled with anticipation and felt her panties in danger of getting wet from the juices starting to flow.

Jessica pulled back from Sam for a moment, and he cupped her chin and placed his mouth on hers, and their tongues met and swirled together, each tasting the other. Jessica unbuttoned Sam's aloha shirt and swept it off his muscular shoulders, then reached down to where his rock-hard heaviness lay against her.

At the same time, Sam unzipped her jeans, pulling them down. He grasped her bottom with both hands and pulled her closer to him.

And again he was pressed firmly against her vulva. He gently pushed her back onto the king-sized bed and slid on top of her, and they pressed their hips together in rhythm. He would not enter her yet, although she begged for him to do so, as he wanted to drive her insane with anticipation.

Sam pulled away from her mouth and took Jessica's hard nipple into his mouth, teasing it slowly with his tongue as she breathed heavily. Then he kissed his way down her stomach to her most private place and ran his tongue up and down, inserting a finger to apply pressure on her most sensitive spot as he circled it with his tongue and flicked it up and down in rapid succession.

Jessica spasmed and wildly bucked her hips as Sam kept the pressure on her with his tongue. Finally, she couldn't stand it anymore and gently grabbed his head and pulled him up to meet her lips. They locked tongues again and kissed passionately. She wanted every inch of him in her now.

After he slid back up on top of her and their lips met, he thrust into her, and she wrapped her legs around him and moaned in ecstasy as he drove her into the bed with each thrust of his hips. Jessica dug her fingers into Sam's back, and he cupped her bottom with his hands so he could control her as he buried himself in her with long, slow strokes that built to a frenzy that ended in Sam emptying himself in Jessica as they both came to orgasm at the same time.

Sam leaned over Jessica, resting on his elbows as they were joined together. He tried to catch his breath for a moment, then rolled over next to her and collapsed. They held each other, savoring the moment as they listened to the thunder outside and the fast-moving tropical downpour bouncing rain off the tender's deck.

Out of the blue, Sam asked her about the tattoo of the three Japanese characters on her right shoulder blade. She lay with her back to him, and he traced his fingertips lightly over the emblems inked into her skin, causing her to shiver. It had been a long time since a man's touch had had that effect on Jessica.

"It was a mistake I made a long time ago. I was sixteen or seventeen at the time and lied about my age to the tattoo artist."

Jessica didn't want to talk about it and got up to put her clothes back on.

"Whoa, whoa, whoa. Don't run off. What does it mean?"

Jessica stopped for a moment, holding her bra. "It represents false heroes and poor choices in my life at the time." Sam could see it bothered her to talk about it.

"So you're not perfect after all." Sam sighed and then smiled. "I thought I was the only one with a few skeletons in the closet," he continued. They both laughed and felt an easing of the momentary tension.

"You, Mr. Successful, have skeletons? Oh, do tell," Jessica teased.

Before Sam could answer, Jessica's phone rang. It was Uncle Jack.

Jessica covered the phone for a second before answering it, looking into Sam's eyes and smiling. "I want skeletons when I get off the phone." Then she answered the phone. "Hey, Uncle."

It was the first time Jessica had sounded happy to Uncle Jack in a long time.

"I don't know what you're doing to sound so chipper, but you should keep it up. I was calling to see if you're still coming," said Uncle Jack.

Jessica laughed. "We're almost there."

11

GOLF PRO

J in listened to Jack Murphy's message while he was on his way to eat dinner with his ninety-four-year-old father, Eizō. They met every week to talk about yakuza business. His father was the original yakuza boss who had started the gang in Hawaii. The meeting always took place at a little out-of-the-way diner in downtown Honolulu that had the best saimen in town.

While Jin was the boss of the yakuza in Hawaii, Eizō insisted Jin call Lance Ishikawa in Kona, the yakuza's enforcer on the big island. For the most part, the yakuza had a strict hands-off policy regarding the outer islands, except for a few nefarious activities here and there that involved the Kona cops. Until now. This was family the Triads had messed with, and now it was time to send them a message. A dead body should get their attention.

Mr. Lau was hosting a critical golf tournament at the Ming and was sending his chauffeur to meet the plane of Dai Yan, a golf pro from Shanghai that Mr. Lau had personally invited to play in the tournament. Dai Yan was a very famous and influential golfer in China and could send a lot of business to the Ming if he liked the resort and its golf course.

Lance Ishikawa parked alongside the road leaving the Ming, propping the hood to his Sprinter van open to make it look like he had engine trouble. The vehicle looked like any of the island tour vans that came and went from the Ming. Except it wasn't. It was a yakuza murder wagon in disguise. Inside were all the tools necessary to dispose of a body without leaving a trace. Jin had taught Lance that the best way to get rid of a body was to put it in a fifty-five-gallon drum, fill it with concrete, and then dump it at sea. If there was no body, then there was no evidence and would be no conviction. This time, though, they would send the body back to Mr. Lau to make a point. It was risky from a prosecution standpoint, but necessary so that there was no mistaking the message they were sending the Triads.

When the Ming's limousine passed by Lance, he closed the hood, hopped in the Sprinter and followed the car to the Kona airport. The limo had parked in the cell phone lot, waiting for the golfer's plane to land. Lance parked right next to the limo and watched the driver for two minutes before making his move. The chauffeur was still looking down at his phone when Lance walked up to the driver's-side window and reached in with a stun gun. He stuck it to the chauffeur's neck and pulled the trigger, then pulled him out of the limo, opened the side door of the Sprinter and threw him on the floor.

After gagging and zip-tying the driver, Lance grabbed the man's cell phone and got in the limo, waiting for the call to pick the golf pro up at the curb. Thirty minutes later, Dai Yan was in the back of the limo and heading towards certain death.

Lance drove to the southernmost part of the airport, past where all the private jets parked, and pulled the limo over. Dai Yan was in the back of the car talking on his cell phone and didn't notice what was going on. Lance walked to the rear passenger-side door of the limo, opened it and stabbed

Dai Yan in the chest with an ice pick he pulled out of his back pocket. Yan was dead seconds after the pick perforated his heart.

Lance took the limo back to the cell phone lot and drugged the chauffeur before putting him back in the limo. He went back to the Sprinter and left the parking lot.

❀

MR. LAU HAD BEEN in his office talking on the phone with Governor Fitch about what to do concerning Aloha Village when his secretary burst into the room and handed him a bloody note.

Dai Yan had a message pinned to his chest that said, "Next time it's your wife. Then it will be you. The best thing you can do is get back on your private jet and go back to Hong Kong where you came from."

It was evident to Mr. Lau that someone connected to Jessica Kealoha had murdered Dai Yan. Mr. Lau had made a dangerous enemy when he'd told Woo Ching to kill her. What Lau didn't know was that Jessica's uncle and grandfather were the leaders of the Japanese mob in Hawaii, and they would have no qualms about killing anyone who threatened their family. The yakuza owned Hawaii, and the Triads had not only tried to kill Jessica, but they were trespassing and would be punished for it.

There were no secrets on the big island, and it didn't take Mr. Lau long to find out that Jessica was connected to the yakuza by blood. Even though she was a former cop, the yakuza would protect her because she was family. Mr. Lau knew he had made a formidable enemy now and would have to deal with it. The first thing he did was to call Woo Ching. Mr. Lau knew Woo Ching had not left the island yet, and he would need him for personal security until this situation with Jessica and the yakuza was over.

"There's a change in plans. I need you to finish the job."

"What do you want me to do?" Woo Ching asked.

"I still need Jessica Kealoha dead."

Woo Ching was glad his uncle had decided to let him try again. The smile on his face said it all. This time he would not fail.

Even though Mr. Lau was a relative newcomer to the island and was there to build a mega gambling resort once gambling became legal, he was Chinese, and they had roots on the island going back to the 1800s, just like the Japanese. And just like in World War Two, they would fight it out again, but this time it would be a gang war between the two sides. The Triads had about twenty members in Kona, and Mr. Lau thought they could handle the yakuza, who he knew had little presence on the big island. What he didn't realize was that that was about to change.

THE NEXT DAY Eizō and Jin met again at the small diner to plan the next step in kicking the Triads out of Hawaii.

Eizō asked Jin, "Lance sent the message?"

"Yes."

"Good."

Eizō stared down into his bowl as he sipped the last of his saimen, then looked up at Jin. "The Triads are tough. Don't underestimate them. They won't go until we make it too uncomfortable for them to stay. And if they've decided Jessica must die, they won't stop until she is dead, or we've convinced them otherwise."

Jin nodded, stirring soy sauce into a small dab of wasabi. "Or until we kill every last one of them."

Eizō nodded in agreement. "Jin, I know you and Jessica have had differences in the past. But she's still my grand-daughter. The Kona cops can't protect her. It's up to us."

Even though Eizō had handed the day-to-day operations of the yakuza over to Jin years before, Eizō still had the final say about anything related to yakuza business in Hawaii. Jin never questioned the orders of his father, who spent most of his days tending to his prize-winning koi.

"Get the crews together and go to Kona. That Chinese bastard won't go without a fight," said Eizō as he slid his bowl of saimen away with a look of disgust on his face.

"*Hai!*" answered Jin.

The yakuza had a fleet of fishing boats they operated out of Oahu. Jin sent the biggest one of them which had a crew of twenty-three men. That was all he would need to teach the Triads a lesson.

SAM'S TENDER dropped him and Jessica off at the fuel dock at Honokohau Harbor, and they walked over to the *Hui Hou*'s slip to borrow Uncle Jack's truck. As usual, Jack was sitting in the fighting chair, reading *Fish News* and puffing on a cigar, when Sam and Jessica walked down the dock.

Jack put the cigar out and got up, grabbing a small backpack he'd gotten ready for Jessica out of the saloon. He brought it out to the cockpit and set it in the fighting chair.

"You guys look good for people who almost got blown up today." Uncle Jack smiled.

"Nothing like a bomb first thing in the morning to get your day started off right," Sam joked. Jessica cut her eyes towards Sam. It was apparent she didn't see the humor in it.

Uncle Jack picked his cigar back up, relit it and took a drag. "After you called me, I thought about how the bomb was made and came to the conclusion it was made with chemicals bought without suspicion." Jessica nodded in agreement. She knew where Jack was going with this, and Sam did too. Though Sam wasn't in law enforcement, he was a smart guy, and his first thought had been of the Oklahoma City bombing. A fertilizer bomb.

Uncle Jack handed Jessica a surveillance photo of Woo Ching. Jessica knew the next step to take after going to the bank to deposit the check from Auntie Loana. A trip to the farm supply store to see if anyone who worked there recognized the photo.

"There's a Smith & Wesson Slim Nine in the bag and ten paper targets to keep the cops from arresting you for concealed carry. Just remember, you're on the way to target practice." Uncle Jack winked.

Smiling at Uncle Jack, Jessica grabbed the bag with one hand and held out her other.

"Oops, sorry. Here's the keys to my old Ford. You can't miss it. It's parked over there." Uncle Jack pointed east towards the parking lot in front of the Fishing Club building, about a hundred yards from the *Hui Hou*.

Uncle Jack had a blue-and-white '67 Ford Bronco with a 351 Cleveland engine. Jessica was always excited to drive her dad and Uncle Jack's vehicles. They both had to drive something that was fast. She figured they were both a couple of adrenaline junkies that got off on going a hundred and thirty miles an hour down the Queen K when nobody was around. Just thinking about it produced a flash memory of how her dad would take her to the Hilo drag strip and let her race his Road Runner when she was sixteen. By the time Jessica had turned seventeen, she had been a feared bracket racer at the track, regularly proving that women had faster reflexes than men. All things being equal, she would win nine times out of ten.

Uncle Jack's Bronco looked like an old piece of crap, just the way he liked it. He never had to worry about anybody banging into it in a parking lot. Even though the paint job had faded and it had primer grey covering the previous rust spots, it was in fair condition from outward appearances. In street racer jargon, it was a sleeper. Under the hood was a custom-built street/strip dyno-tuned engine that put out an easy five hundred horsepower to the ground. According to Uncle Jack, it ran like a striped-assed ape.

Sam strapped in, sitting shotgun, and Jessica fired up the big Ford engine and pointed the rocket disguised as a Bronco towards the bank in town so they could deposit the check that would save Aloha Village.

AFTER DEPOSITING Auntie Loana's check for one point two million dollars, Jessica called Jasmine to let her know Aloha Village could pay bills without worry now, and that she and Sam were on their way to find out who'd tried to kill them earlier that day.

Sam and Jessica walked into the farm supply store and showed the photo to the young man working that day. The clerk remembered seeing Woo Ching in the store because he had been wearing a suit. At the time, the clerk had thought it was strange to sell fertilizer to a guy in a suit.

Sam and Jessica thanked the clerk and headed back to the harbor to return Uncle Jack's Bronco.

Sam asked Jessica. "What do you think?"

"Let's find Woo Ching and hope he forces me to put a bullet in him."

Sam looked horrified.

Then she laughed. "I'm just kidding. Sort of. Okay, not," she said with a passive aggressive tone.

"How about we go talk to the Kona PD instead, before going back to the harbor?" Sam suggested.

Jessica knew Sam was right. If they were on the mainland, that would be the right way to handle things. But Jessica feared that talking to the Kona cops would the same as discussing it with Mr. Lau himself because of spies in the department. She decided to talk to them anyway. But Jessica would only speak to Sid Akiona, her old partner. He was the only one she trusted there. When she had been accused of theft as a young rookie, Sid was the only one who'd stood up for her. He had known for a fact she didn't steal fifty thousand dollars out of the police evidence room. At the time, it was still an old boys' club and women had not been welcome in the department. Any way they could get rid of a woman was okay with most of the upper echelon, and Jessica was no exception.

Everyone knew the theft allegation was a ruse; she had made a powerful enemy when she had written the chief of police a ticket for being parked in a red zone at a local hotel, where he'd had a nooner with his mistress. Even the internal affairs detectives investigating the missing money had known Jessica didn't do it. But she was being blamed by a senior officer who was the brother-in-law of the chief. There was talk around the station that one of the evidence room workers had stolen the money, but charges had never been filed. And Jessica was the scapegoat they'd tried to pin it on, since she had been the last one in the room before the theft was discovered. Jessica had gotten cleared after six months of investigation, but it was evident to her that the stink of the accusation would never go away. That was when she'd quit and moved to LA, so she could go to work for a big-city police department where nepotism wasn't allowed.

12

KONA PD

S am and Jessica parked the Bronco far enough away from the entrance to the police station so that nobody inside the building would see what she and Sam were doing while seated in the Bronco. Uncle Jack had a custom-built gun safe built into the floor of the Bronco, and Jessica put the Smith & Wesson Slim Nine inside it and locked the door. No need to test out Uncle's target practice excuse story, she thought.

Sam and Jessica walked through the front double glass doors and up to the desk sergeant. "Is Officer Sid Akiona on shift today?" Jessica asked the young policeman behind the counter.

"Yes, the watch commander is in his office, I believe. Let me see for sure. Who should I tell him is here to see him?"

"Tell him Jessica Kealoha."

A few minutes later, the young policeman returned with Sid Akiona, who was now Captain Akiona. Sid's face lit up with a welcoming smile when he saw Jessica. He was genuinely glad to see her. It had been close to twenty years since the last time they had seen each other. After a warm embrace, Jessica introduced Sam, and he shook Captain

Akiona's hand, though he wasn't crazy about the way the captain looked at Jessica, like they had once been more than just coworkers. It was a weird feeling Sam couldn't seem to shake while they were talking.

"I heard about your father, Jessica. I'm so sorry for your loss," said Captain Akiona.

"Thank you. The reason we're here today is that someone tried to blow us up two days ago with a roadside bomb planted near the exit of Aloha Village. It exploded about sixty yards from us. We were lucky no one was injured."

Captain Akiona's face was expressionless as Sam and Jessica recounted the harrowing details of how they'd almost lost their lives and how they suspected Woo Ching.

Jessica also mentioned that she and Sam had gone to the farm supply store to see if Woo Ching had been there to buy fertilizer and that they suspected it was what was used to make the bomb with. And that they found a clerk who positively identified Woo Ching purchasing a bag of fertilizer from a photo they showed him.

Captain Akiona looked puzzled and then asked, "Where did you get the photo of the guy?"

"My uncle, Jack Murphy."

"You think this Woo Ching is responsible?" asked Captain Akiona.

Jessica nodded. "If it's not him, then it was probably Mother Teresa."

"I see you haven't lost your keen sense of humor. We'll start looking for this guy, and if we find him, we'll bring him in for a chat and see if we can make a case."

Sam and Jessica both shook the captain's hand and thanked him for his time. Then Sam asked one question before they left.

"What's the chances of getting a concealed carry permit these days?"

Jessica already knew the answer but stood by patiently, knowing what the reply would be.

Captain Akiona shook his head. "The chief won't issue them. Never has and said he never will."

"Even if we're in danger?" asked Sam.

"The chief is adamant about not having civilians walking around carrying guns."

"Interesting." Sam shook his head in disbelief.

Jessica smiled and thanked the captain for his time again, then grabbed Sam's hand and steered him towards the door.

As Sam and Jessica drove out of the police station parking lot, Sam looked at Jessica. "Maybe I'm wrong, but I felt an underlying tension between you and Captain Akiona back there. Did you and the good captain have something going on once upon a time?"

Jessica steered the Bronco onto the Queen K Highway to head back towards the harbor, and Sam reached down to unlock the gun safe as he waited for her to answer. She kept her eyes on the road and finally answered, "Let's just say that when we were partners on the night shift, he wanted to be naked partners too. But I wasn't interested." She placed her right hand on Sam's thigh.

Sam felt jealous just thinking about another man wanting Jessica. But her hand on his thigh made the jealous thoughts fade away, and he felt warm inside.

Sam's phone buzzed in his pocket, and he looked down to see who the text was from.

"Why don't we stay on my boat until this is over? I got a text that *The Racer* has arrived and anchored in Kailua Bay."

Jessica didn't hesitate. "I can't leave Jasmine alone. I know she's safe with your guys there in the Village, but I have to go back to the resort until this is over."

Sam sighed, but he understood where she was coming from. "Okay, back to the Village we go. I'll call the tender to pick us up at the harbor after we return the Bronco."

Jessica looked at Sam and smiled. "Since your guys have taken over your bungalow, you'll have to stay with me at mine."

Sam grinned. "Well, if you insist." And they both laughed.

❀

THE *SASHIMI MARU* had been trolling the Kona coast for the past few days. It appeared to be a Japanese fishing boat like any other. Except what wasn't obvious was that it belonged to the yakuza. It was the biggest tuna boat they ran out of Oahu, and besides catching fish, it was a tool used to launder money. And now its crew was plotting their attack on the Triads. With a crew of twenty-three, they had no fear of the Triads outnumbering them.

Their plan was simple: go ashore at night and burn Mr. Lau's villa to the ground while he slept. The worst-case scenario was that he survived the fire. But the fire should be enough to convince him that staying in Kona would be hazardous to his health, and he should go back to China. And the best-case scenario was that he died in the fire, and the Triads in Hong Kong would know Hawaii was forbidden turf, and if they ever came back, they'd would pay with their lives.

It was about three thirty in the morning when Jin Tanaka sent ten guys ashore in the *Sashimi Maru*'s motor launch. They had ten five-gallon gas cans and a box of flares. The yakuza didn't blow things up. They specialized in extortion, prostitution and smuggling guns from Hawaii to Japan. Burning down the Ming was not something they would do without serious provocation, but the Triads had attempted to kill two of the granddaughters of Eizō Tanaka, and the yakuza would make them pay the price for their transgression.

Jin Tanaka told his guys where to find Mr. Lau's villa on the grounds and made it clear that they weren't to burn any part of the Ming where guests were staying. The yakuza would kill when they had to, but killing innocent people like tourists was not good for business and would bring the feds in force. Killing the leader of the Triads in Hawaii would most likely only bring a local response, and it would be lukewarm at best. Jin Tanaka had men on the payroll throughout the state government and the Kona PD and would be able to control the investigation, as he had in the past.

By 5:15 a.m., Jin Tanaka could see the glow of Mr. Lau's Villa engulfed in flames. Jin was smoking a cigarette topside of the *Sashimi Maru* while he watched Mr. Lau's Villa burn to the ground through his binoculars. *Good riddance*, he thought. Around the time the sun was coming up, the glow subsided.

As the group of Japanese thugs headed back towards the motor launch at the beach, they came across a wild goat that had been munching grass on the golf course. They killed it and threw it in the resort's swimming pool as a message to the Triads that they'd best be planning on leaving Hawaii.

When the fire department arrived on scene at the Ming, Mr. Lau's villa was destroyed. There was nothing left to save. What Jin Tanaka didn't know was that Lau wasn't there. He had been staying in one of the resort's guest rooms because he feared retaliation from the yakuza. And rightly so.

THE YAKUZA HAD a spy working at the Ming that Jin Tanaka had been checking in with during his weekly visits to take Kainoa to the beach. Jin liked taking Kainoa to the beach, but his weekly visits to the big island were about a lot more than just being a good uncle. Figuring out what the Triads were up to had been his number one goal for the past six months. China White fentanyl was what they were up to, besides trying to get gambling legalized and take over Aloha Village.

The yakuza had known the Triads had been shipping

fentanyl to the big island and hadn't cared. Until now. The yakuza had been planning to rip off the drugs for some time and decided this would be the perfect time to kill two birds with one stone. Lance Ishikawa was waiting with the murder wagon to take five of the ten men sent ashore to the Triads' body shop to steal the drugs while the other five were busy burning down Mr. Lau's villa at the Ming.

Jin Tanaka's inside man at the Ming kept seeing exotic high-end European cars being shipped to the resort in a container from Hong Kong every month. Jin figured the Triads were hiding drugs in the vehicles, and sending them in containers made it almost impossible for drug-sniffing dogs to catch them.

Once the car arrived, Mr. Lau would have Woo Ching take the vehicle to a body shop the Triads owned in the old industrial area to have it dismantled and painted. Afterward, the cars would be shipped to the mainland and sold at auction. Financially, it made little sense. The vehicles cost more in Hong Kong than they did in the US, and it cost more to ship them to Hawaii—unless they were carrying two or three kilos of China White hidden inside them.

Jin Tanaka had no desire to go into the business of selling dope. Hookers, guns, and extortion were okay, but drugs were taboo to the yakuza. But the way he saw it, this was free money. He would dump the fentanyl at a discount to move it fast and donate some of the proceeds to a drug rehab center on the island.

❀

THE HAPPY COUPLE was sitting on the lanai, having their morning coffee after a long night of hot sex, when Jessica's phone rang. It was Uncle Jack.

"Just a heads-up—the cops will come to see you soon."

"Why?"

"They got called to the Ming a few days ago about a dead Chinese golfer. He was found in the back of their limousine at the airport. They think it was a professional hit, from the intelligence I've got. The limo driver told the cops a wild story about being abducted and then waking up back in the limousine later with the dead guy in the backseat. My source says at first the cops weren't buying it, but then there was a witness who corroborated his story, saying he saw the limo driver get stuffed back into the car from a van that parked right next to it."

"Why does the Kona PD want to talk to me?"

"My source says Mr. Lau told them you would do anything to disrupt his business and might somehow be connected to the murder and burning down his villa."

Jessica's forehead wrinkled. "Figures. Thanks for the heads-up."

"I guess he thinks if he can't kill you, he'll try to get you locked up. Oh, one last thing. Be careful."

"Something I ought to know?" Jessica asked.

"That's all I can say right now." Then Uncle Jack hung up the phone.

I hate it when he pulls that secret agent shit on me, she thought. And then she jumped up from the table where they had been sitting and stomped on a centipede about five times. It had slithered out of a puka in the rock staircase that led to the lanai.

Sam couldn't see it because the table was between the two of them and blocked his view of the prehistoric-looking creature that was about six inches long and had what looked like a thousand legs all moving at once. At first he thought she was overreacting to Uncle Jack on the phone and was taking it out on the lanai by stomping her foot.

"Take that, you son of a bitch," Jessica said as she ground what remained of the centipede's head into the wood flooring of the lanai.

Sam peered over the edge of the table.

"Yup, you killed the shit out of him." And they both laughed.

"Literally," she replied.

"Feel better?"

"Yes, I do."

WHEN DETECTIVE GOMES showed up at Aloha Village, Sam and Jessica were on stand-up paddle boards in the middle of the bay fronting the resort. Jessica had been trying to lose the ten pounds she'd gained. That was the thing about being back in Hawaii—potato mac and two scoops of rice always came with the plate lunch, and a zillion carbs to boot. Until her thirties, she could eat anything and not gain an ounce. After forty, just looking at a chocolate cake seemed to equal gaining five pounds. And since her father's death, she'd been hitting the chocolate cake hard the last couple of weeks.

Coffee, booze, cigarettes, and donuts used to be Jessica's four major food groups; now she was just down to sugar. It was a reasonable compromise in her mind. Besides, unlike booze, nobody ever got arrested for eating cake.

Detective Gomes never met a malasada he didn't like, and he sat down at the aloha bar overlooking the bay and helped himself to a box of the tasty Portuguese treats the resort had put out that morning for guests. He ate the whole box of them while he waited for Sam and Jessica to paddle back in. At three hundred and thirty pounds and gaining, Gomes's motto was "Eat until you're tired, not until you're full."

Jessica didn't recognize Gomes from her early days on the force, but he remembered her, and the allegations made against her years earlier when she was with the Kona PD. Gomes didn't care one way or the other about Jessica being a dirty cop, but he doubted she'd had anything to do with the murder of the golf pro.

"Ms. Kealoha, if you have a few minutes, I'd like a word." He introduced himself and handed her his card. Jessica glanced at it.

"How can I help you, Detective?"

"Can you account for your whereabouts yesterday?"

Sam interjected, "She was with me."

"And you are?" Gomes asked.

"I'm Sam Stewart. We were here all day yesterday, laying on the beach and snorkeling. Plenty of the staff here at the resort saw us."

Gomes was looking down at his notebook and nodding as he wrote down Sam's name.

"I think this should do it," said Gomes. And that was it. He found one more malasada in the box on the bar and ate it on the way back to his car. Sam and Jessica never heard another word from Detective Gomes.

13

A WEEK LATER

The Kona PD had been looking for Woo Ching for close to a week and had come up empty. Jessica was tired of waiting. It would be up to her and Sam to bring Woo Ching to justice.

Jessica knew they had a spy at Aloha Village feeding info to Mr. Lau. How else would the Triads have known she was on her way to the bank to deposit a check to save the Village the day Woo Ching tried to blow them up? Jessica knew someone had tipped them off and decided she would use the mole to set a trap for Woo Ching. What Sam and Jessica didn't know was that Woo Ching was busy setting a trap of his own that would preempt their plan.

BESIDES WORKING part-time for her dad at the Village, Jasmine was a massage therapist and had had a side business at Aloha Village the past couple of years while going to college to become a veterinarian someday. And she was taking care of Sam's cat, Mr. Jangles while Sam's house at Keauhou Bay was in escrow. She was a busy girl. That was the thing about Mike

Murphy's daughters—they were all hard workers and always tried to get ahead financially.

So when Jasmine's phone rang and it was a new client asking to schedule a massage, she thought nothing of it. She agreed to meet at two o'clock that afternoon at the beach massage cabana. Between the resort's guests and word of mouth, Jasmine didn't need to advertise for business, but she always asked who had referred the new client so she could send them a thank-you card for the referral. Woo Ching had used a common Japanese surname when Jasmine had asked him who referred him to her. She had two clients with that same name and thought she would figure out which one it was when she met her new client at two p.m.

Sam's security team had a photo of Wu Ching and had been warned to be on the lookout for him. But Woo Ching was a master of disguise. He put on a wig and a fake beard, and when he showed up for the two o'clock massage, he looked like a harmless old man. Nobody recognized him, and he had booked under a phony name. He knew Sam's security team was in the Village and that he would have to trick Jasmine into walking him to his car in the parking lot, where he would drug and abduct her.

During the massage, Jasmine mentioned she would be a veterinarian someday. Woo Ching tuned in on that as the weakness he would exploit to get her to walk out to his car. He told her about his new poi dog puppy that didn't seem to act right and wanted to show it to her to get her opinion about what was wrong with him. Dragging her out of the resort would never work. But if he could trick Jasmine into walking to the parking lot of her own free will, she was as good as gone.

Jasmine and what appeared to be an old man strolled to the parking lot arm in arm, and when security offered to escort them, Jasmine waved them off. "No need."

Hours later, Jasmine woke up groggy and with a headache

from the drug-induced state she had been in. She was lying on a concrete floor in the fetal position in a room that was only eight feet wide by eight feet long, with plywood walls and a low plywood ceiling. The roof wasn't even high enough to allow Jasmine to stand up inside the box. Woo Ching had padlocked her inside the makeshift prison at a warehouse in the old industrial area. The only thing she remembered was leaning in the window of the old man's car to look at the dog. As soon as she'd leaned in, Woo Ching had pulled a rag with chloroform out of his pocket and smothered her face with it.

The warehouse belonged to Mr. Lau. It was in a row of them he owned, and at the very end of the road behind a locked gate. Jasmine yelled for help, but it wasn't coming. Woo Ching had set up a camera in the room and kept her under surveillance with an app on his phone, and it had a two-way speaker built-in.

"You're wasting your time screaming for help. No one can hear you. You're inside a building that is soundproof, and there is no one around," the voice said to Jasmine through a speaker mounted on the ceiling of the box she was being held prisoner in.

"Who are you? What do you want? Please, let me out of here," Jasmine cried.

"I want your sister. And you're the bait," answered the voice.

Jasmine quit crying. "You know she'll kill you for this, right?"

There was no reply from the voice on the other end of the speaker.

Woo Ching had taken Jasmine's phone when she was unconscious and found Jessica's phone number, and then he had thrown the phone out the window on the way to the building. He knew Jessica would check the phone records to see the cell tower location of the last ping from Jasmine's phone to get an idea where she might be. But Jessica wouldn't need to figure it out. If Jessica didn't do what Woo Ching asked, he would tell her where to find Jasmine. Dead.

❀

THE NEXT DAY, Woo Ching called Jessica from a burner phone. Since she didn't recognize the number, she let it go to voicemail.

Momi was the front desk clerk at Aloha Village that day and got a strange phone call that sent shivers down her spine, and she called Jessica immediately after the call.

When Jessica answered her phone, she had a hard time understanding Momi, who was in tears as she tried to tell Jessica that a man had called the front desk and said he had taken Jasmine and he was holding her hostage and that if Jessica didn't do as he said, he would kill her.

"Take a breath, Momi, and then tell me what he said to you."

"He said to tell you to check your voicemail, and if you ever want to see her again, you better answer your phone when he calls again." Jessica felt a pang of fear as she asked Momi about Jasmine's schedule before she'd disappeared.

"She had a massage client yesterday at two pm, and nobody has seen her since that time, but she had a college class afterward, so nobody thought anything about it," Momi said.

Sam was sitting on the lanai, working on a proposal for the Hawaii ferry, when he heard Jessica on the phone inside the bungalow and could tell from her side of the conversation and the tone of her voice that something was wrong. After Jessica hung up, he set his laptop down on the table and asked her, "What happened?"

"Jasmine has been kidnapped! I'm going to go find the man responsible for this."

"We," Sam interjected.

"Okay, we have to go look for her." Jessica grabbed her thigh holster off the kitchen counter and slipped it over her right leg under her sundress, then stuffed the nine-millimeter pistol that Uncle Jack had loaned her in it. In LA, she always wore jeans and carried a backup gun in an ankle holster at work. She almost felt naked without it and mumbled something to that effect, and Sam heard it.

"Not a problem. I'll be back in a few minutes." Sam went to his bungalow, where his security team had set up shop, and returned with two Glock 19s and a couple of extra magazines of ammo. "This should be enough, don't you think?" He handed Jessica one of the Glocks and an extra clip with fifteen rounds in it.

Jessica grabbed her small backpack, put the gun inside, slung it over her shoulder and said, "Let's go."

Jessica fired up the 426 Hemi engine in her father's '69 Road Runner and backed it out of the garage, then got out of the car while the engine warmed up, which was necessary for that cold-blooded beast. She had a look on her face that downright scared the crap out of Sam.

"This is too dangerous," she said. "You don't need to come with me. Besides, if something happened to you, I wouldn't be able to cope with it again."

"Again?" Sam asked

"My first husband and I were on a stakeout one night," Jessica started, and then her phone rang.

"This is Jessica Kealoha," she answered quickly.

"Your sister will die if you don't do what I tell you," the voice on the other end said in broken English.

"Okay, what do you want?"

Sam could tell the rumble of the big Hemi engine was making it hard to hear, so he shut it down while Jessica was on the phone.

"We want our merchandise back," the caller said.

"I don't understand what the hell you're talking about."

"The yakuza ripped us off is what I'm talking about."

It became crystal-clear to Jessica right at that moment what had happened. She needed no further explanation.

"If I can get your drugs back, you'll let my sister go?"

"That's the deal, lady. There will be a cigarette boat at VV buoy at six p.m tonight. Show up with our ten kilos, and we'll release your sister after the drop. If you bring Five-O with you, your sister is dead." And the phone went dead.

Jessica had put Woo Ching on speaker so Sam could hear the whole conversation. Jessica was mentally tough, but this was almost too much, and Sam could see her eyes well up with tears as she walked back inside the bungalow.

"If we call the FBI, they could—"

Jessica cut Sam off and held up her hand. "We're not. I know who to call. The only way this works out is if the Triads get their drugs back."

Sam thought better of arguing with her. Besides, she was more of an expert at this sort of thing than him. All he knew was how to build super yachts. Jessica was the expert at dealing with criminals. But Sam was an expert when it came to risk assessment. And this situation looked as risky as swimming with sharks to him.

For the first time in three years, Jessica wanted to pour herself a gin and tonic and think about the whole thing. But that choice was no longer available to her, so she did the next best thing. She went to the bathroom so Sam couldn't hear and called her grandfather, Eizō Tanaka, over in Honolulu.

"Hi, Grandpa. It's Jessica."

"Jasmine has been taken hostage by the Triads. They want their dope back or they'll kill her."

"I'll make a phone call," Eizō Tanaka said, and he hung up the phone.

Jessica walked back into the living room and sat down on the couch, exhaling a guarded sigh of relief.

Sam sat next to her and rested his hand on her leg. "Why

don't you want to call the FBI? I don't get it. We're talking about Jasmine's life and stolen drugs, and you don't want their help. What the hell am I missing here?"

"There's not enough time. The nearest office is in Honolulu, and by the time they get here, it'll be too late. There won't be enough agents, and the Triads will kill Jasmine before the FBI has a game plan. The other reason is my family. I guess now is as good a time as any to bring out the skeletons. You'll never want to see me again after you hear this."

Jessica stood up and paced back and forth in the living room for a minute before she said another word.

"I know who has the Triads' dope. It's one of my uncles on my mother's side of the family." And then she paused for a moment. "You know the tattoo you asked me about? It means yakuza. Three of my uncles on my mother's side are yakuza gang members. My grandfather on my mother's side is the founder of the yakuza in Hawaii."

Sam said nothing and just listened as Jessica shared one of her deepest, darkest secrets. The shame was written all over her face.

Sam stood up from the couch and walked over to Jessica, wrapping his arms around her. "I've got skeletons too," he whispered in her ear.

IT HAD BEEN six hours since Jessica had called her grandfather, and she had heard nothing. She and Sam were sitting at the dining room table, cleaning their guns to pass the time while they waited to find out where the Triads' stolen drugs were so they could make the trade for Jasmine.

Jessica had a view straight out the window and saw Pua's Mercedes coming up the driveway. Pua had come to the bungalow to get Sam's signature on closing documents for the house he'd bought in Keauhou. She had been negotiating hard the last month to get the deal closed and thought the day would be one of celebration instead of the bad news about Jasmine she was about to get.

After Pua got out of her Mercedes and walked up the steps to the lanai, she could see the grim expressions on both Sam and Jessica's faces through the dining room window.

"Did someone die, or is someone going to?" Pau said in a half-kidding tone of voice as she eyeballed both of them focusing on the guns and not her.

Jessica kept polishing the barrel of the Glock, not making eye contact. "Jasmine's missing. She's been gone about eighteen hours or so."

Pua threw the papers in her hand down on the kitchen table and glared at her older sister. "When did you plan on telling me?"

Jessica had been hoping not to have to tell her until after Jasmine had been rescued; she knew Pua had enough on her plate with having breast cancer and didn't need any additional stress.

"I'm sorry. I was hoping to have Jasmine back home before you found out."

"Why are you sitting here and not out trying to get her back?"

Jessica stuck the Glock 19 in her ankle holster. "We're waiting for Uncle Jin to call and tell us where we can find the ransom so we can exchange it for Jasmine."

"How much do they want?" Pua asked.

"It's not money they want. And the less you know about it, the better," Jessica said.

Pua had done enough shady real estate deals over the years to know when to quit asking questions, and she recognized this was one of those times, even though it wasn't related to property.

Pua was standing there in the kitchen when her phone

rang. She almost never took a call when with a client signing papers, and Sam was the most significant client she'd ever had. But when she saw it was Uncle Jin, she picked up.

"Uncle," she answered.

Jessica reached out towards Pua. "I want to talk to him," she said firmly.

Pua ignored Jessica and turned away from her. "I'm here with Sam and Jessica. I'll tell them." And then she hung up the phone.

Jessica's nostrils flared, and her brow furrowed when Pua didn't hand her the phone.

"He said you'd find what you're looking for on board Uncle's fishing boat at the harbor."

The anger left Jessica just as fast as it had come. "Let's go," she barked, and they piled into Pua's Mercedes and raced to the harbor. To protect Pua, she and Sam never told her what was on the fishing boat, and Pua was smart enough not to ask.

Jin Tanaka's forty-five-foot Hatteras was in its slip with the key in it and not a soul around when Pua dropped Sam and Jessica off at the harbor. It had been a long time since Jessica handled such a big yacht, and she decided the smart thing to do was let Sam take the helm, since he had a lot more experience handling big boats than she did. As they walked to the slip, Sam remarked, "Nice boat."

"And who said crime doesn't pay?" Jessica muttered. "It's going straight to the bottom if we don't get Jasmine back. And I might sink it anyway."

"Could you not sink it while I'm on board?" Sam asked in a joking kind of way, trying to ease the tension.

"We'll see," Jessica said with a half smile.

Sam fired up the big Caterpillar engines, Jessica cast off the lines, and they idled out of Honokohau Harbor towards the open sea. Jessica had fished these waters with her father when she was growing up and knew them well enough to point Sam in the right direction towards VV buoy, where the exchange was supposed to take place. The buoy was only about four miles offshore of Kailua Bay.

And spotting a cigarette boat would be easy, since they were a rare boat in Hawaiian waters.

As they approached the buoy, Jessica had binoculars pointed at the horizon, looking for any fast-approaching boats. Nothing. It was almost six p.m. The dope was in a duffle bag lying next to the fighting chair at the rear of the boat.

A few minutes later, a thirty-eight-foot Top Gun cigarette boat approached the Hatteras from the north at a high rate of speed. "That thing must be going over eighty knots. If you planned on chasing them down after getting Jasmine back, that's not happening," Sam said.

"I just want her safely on board. I'll look for Woo Ching later, after we get Jasmine back to Aloha Village," Jessica replied.

Sam and Jessica checked their guns and then reholstered them with the safeties off, ready to rock if they had to. Jessica had eyes on Woo Ching through her binoculars and could see Jasmine seated at the back of the boat with her hands bound behind her back. Her waist-length dark brown hair was blowing in the wind. Jasmine was less than a quarter of a mile away from being freed. A radio call from the Coast Guard came over the VHF marine radio on the Hatteras and jolted Sam and Jessica out of their focus on Jasmine. They hadn't even noticed the Coast Guard response boat that had come upon them from behind out of the south and wanted to board the Hatteras.

"You've got to be kidding me," Sam said.

"Quick, hide the guns and the dope," Jessica ordered Sam. "I'll stall them." Jessica clicked the safety back on and handed Sam her Glock, hoping the Coast Guard crew didn't see the handoff with binoculars.

As soon as Woo Ching saw the flashing blue light of the Coast Guard response boat, he hooked a hard U-turn, opened up the throttle on the Top Gun racer and disappeared into the sunset.

It became evident as the Coast Guard boat approached the Hatteras that this would not be an inspection for lifejackets. Four petty officers were standing at the front of the response boat, holding M4 rifles. They were here looking for drugs, and they meant business. Mr. Lau had set a trap and Sam and Jessica had walked right into it. Mr. Lau was willing to donate ten kilos of China White if it meant Jessica would be behind bars and out of the way.

Jessica pulled her cell phone out and hit the button to dial Uncle Jack. As usual, he didn't answer. "I don't have time to explain. Jasmine was kidnapped and is on a boat heading north from VV buoy. I'd check the Puako boat ramp for a cigarette boat getting pulled out of the water. That's the guy who has her. The Coast Guard will probably arrest me and Sam in a few minutes, and that's why I'm telling you this. Go find the guy with that boat, and you'll find Jasmine." Then she hung up.

The Coast Guard petty officers boarded the Hatteras and searched it until they found the drugs. Jessica and Sam tried to explain that they were trying to exchange them for Jasmine. The petty officer in charge of the boarding party was empathetic and didn't think Sam and Jessica were drug dealers, but it wasn't up to him to let them go. He still had his orders to handcuff them and take them into custody.

By this time, Jessica had nothing to lose by begging the Coast Guard to look for the cigarette boat and Jasmine. Once they found out Jessica was a former LA detective, they took her story seriously and dispatched an HC-130 to look for Jasmine.

Woo Ching's plan had never been to trade Jasmine for the ten kilos of China White. It had always been about getting

Jessica arrested for being in possession of the dope. Mr. Lau had correctly gambled that Jessica wouldn't call the cops or FBI and would try to make the exchange for Jasmine herself. And the gamble had paid off, with Sam and Jessica in federal custody at the detention center in Honolulu.

Woo Ching took Jasmine northwest towards Kohala and was about ten miles offshore when he decided that should be far enough. He had a simple plan. Shoot Jasmine in the head and throw her body over the side.

Jasmine had been a competitive free diver in her late teens and had held her breath as long as five minutes. As soon as Woo Ching brought the boat to a stop and shut off the engines, Jasmine knew it was now or never. She tucked into a ball and brought her arms underneath her feet so she could get her hands in front her. Thank goodness for the yoga class she had taught the last year at the resort, she thought as she performed the maneuver with little effort. Jasmine quickly broke the zip tie using a method her karate teacher showed her, pulling it as tight as possible, then raising her hands over her head and slamming them into her belly.

Woo Ching had his back to Jasmine and wasn't paying attention until she stood up with her arms in front of her and snapped the zip tie he had wrapped around her wrists. As Woo Ching turned toward her, he pulled a snub-nosed .357 Magnum out of his pocket. He brought the gun up to fire, but Jasmine was lightning fast and dove over the back of the boat into the water before he got a round off in her direction.

She only had seconds to hyperventilate before going in the water, but it was enough to allow her to get a big gulp of air. She also knew she risked shallow-water blackout by hyper-ventilating, but it was her only choice. Jasmine had a simple idea. Dive deep and hold her breath long enough to make

Woo Ching think she was dead. Her plan didn't include Woo Ching putting a bullet in her.

Woo Ching fired a half a dozen rounds into the water from the back of the boat. She watched them streak past her like torpedoes. All of them narrowly missed her, except one that struck and passed through her left hand. Jasmine didn't realize she had been shot until she saw the blood in the water.

Jasmine's lungs were burning for air more than she could ever remember. But she knew if she gave in and surfaced, she was dead. Jasmine struggled to stay submerged using the least amount of energy possible. With no weight belt on and her lungs full of air, Jasmine's body wanted to surface as she fought to stay down under the boat. It was simple physics.

After close to four minutes, all Woo Ching saw was blood in the water. He thought for sure she was dead and started up the engines, heading back to the launch ramp at Puako.

When Jasmine couldn't hold her breath another second, she floated to the surface and prayed Woo Ching wouldn't see her. By then, he was a quarter of a mile away and she was safe for the time being.

She had been cupping her left hand as best she could to cover the bullet hole and stop the bleeding as she floated on the surface. She knew if she didn't get the bleeding stopped, sharks would appear soon and end it for her. Jasmine took off her T-shirt, ripped it with her teeth and wrapped a four-inch-wide swath around her hand as a bandage.

Jasmine had trained for the annual Hawaii triathlon for the last two years. She could swim three miles, but she had never swum more than that. If she wanted to live, she'd have to swim three times further than she ever had, and with a bullet hole in her hand. The only thing that kept the pain at bay was the fear of not making it to shore. She wasn't ready to die yet.

It was late in the afternoon, and the ocean surface had light swells about a foot high, with visibility about a hundred feet down. Jasmine could see shadows in the water below her, and out of the deep appeared a big shadow about fourteen feet long. Soon it became clear even without goggles that it was a tiger shark. The blood from Jasmine's wound had attracted it. At least it wasn't acting like it was going into a feeding frenzy, as they were known for doing just before they struck.

It circled Jasmine for about ten minutes, an looking her over as if deciding whether it wanted to have lunch or not. Jasmine was an island girl and had seen sharks before while swimming close to shore. It was no big deal then, because all one had to do was just get out of the water. But this was different. There was nowhere to go. The tiger started to dart back toward Jasmine, and she knew she would die right there as soon as it attacked. Suddenly out of the blue came another shadow from the deep, and then another and another. *Great, he's called his buddies, and now it's going to be over. At least it'll be fast*, she thought.

But this time it wasn't sharks. It was a pod of dolphins, they surrounded Jasmine and formed a barrier between her and the shark. And the shark just as quickly decided to look elsewhere for its lunch.

As Jasmine swam towards the shore, she kept looking toward Mauna Kea so she knew she was going the right direction. But the problem was, the mountain was getting no closer. Only smaller.

She kept telling herself, *You can do this*. But the current was heading towards Japan, and even though she had the stamina to swim ten miles, she couldn't break free of the riptide carrying her away from the island.

The dolphins stayed close to Jasmine, never leaving her alone as she floated on her back for a while to rest and think about what to do next.

Exhausted, she thought how easy it would be just to give up and slide beneath the surface of the ocean. And then she thought of the pain it would cause her sisters, and she wasn't ready to go just yet. She decided she would try swimming two miles south to see if she could get out of the current she was in and then try swimming towards the island.

Jasmine swam south for thirty minutes with everything she had. She still didn't see the island, and it was starting to get dark. She could see the stars becoming visible in the eastern sky. She rolled over on her back again and enjoyed the view before she would die. After an hour, she was almost hypnotized by the beauty of the stars twinkling in the night sky, and she had a good idea that she had drifted a long way from the big island.

Then Jasmine was bumped by a small log that jolted her out of the trance she had put herself in. At least it wasn't a shark, she thought after the initial fear had passed. It was debris from the Japanese tsunami that had made its way to Hawaiian waters. There was a sliver of a moon out, and it provided just enough light that she could see something else bobbing up and down about three hundred feet away.

Jasmine took all the energy she had left and swam to the object. It was a dock that had broken free and floated all the way to Hawaii. It had a rope hanging off one of its cleats into the water. Jasmine barely had the strength to swim to the dock, much less pull herself up on top of it. After resting for ten minutes while hanging on to the rope, she felt she might have the strength to climb the rope.

The pain in her hand was excruciating as she pulled herself up the rope. She wanted to let go, but she knew if she did, she was as good as dead. By the last pull on the line, she reached up and grabbed the cleat and pulled herself all the way up on the dock, where she collapsed, panting and unable to move another inch. She was dehydrated and exhausted, but now she had a chance to live long enough to be found—if she could collect some rainwater before dying of thirst.

AS THE SUN CAME UP, the dolphins reappeared. Not just the ten or twenty that had saved her from the shark the day before, but hundreds of dolphins, if not a thousand.

Great, I've become the dolphin queen, she thought. Then she yelled, "Does anybody have a boat?" and laughed until she cried.

There wasn't a cloud in the sky. The weather had been hot and dry the last week, and the forecast called for more of the same. Jasmine had no protection from the sun and no water. As the hours passed and the sun came overhead, she felt her skin burn, and her tongue felt like it was swelling and turning into leather all at the same time.

Jasmine was the most positive of the three Murphy daughters, but she was finding it hard to be positive about anything other than that she would die of thirst.

I can't control this right now, she thought. *I might as well meditate*. And that was what she did. She cleared her mind and lay on the dock, becoming one with it until she could feel the direction of the ocean swells. Pili Kalea had been the waterman at Aloha Village for many years before he passed, and he had taken all the Murphy sisters out on the water and shared his knowledge of the sea with them. Pili had taught Jasmine well about the sea. He had shown her you could navigate by the stars, and if the weather was cloudy, you could feel the direction you were going in by the ocean's swells.

Jasmine was nowhere near proficient with ancient Hawaiian navigation skills, but she knew enough to tell she was headed towards Molokai, which was a lot better than going to Japan. Still, she didn't let herself get excited. She knew she was much closer to death than she was to living through this nightmare she found herself in.

She sat up straight as soon as she heard the Coast Guard

chopper off in the distance. She prayed it was looking for her, but it was too far away, and there was no way to signal it.

The chopper had been on the scene the maximum amount of time and was low on fuel and made the turn for Oahu. As Jasmine watched it disappear over the horizon, she felt sad to her core. It was over and they would never find her.

She was so focused on watching it fly off that she didn't hear the Coast Guard HC-130 come up behind her from the south. They had been flying over the southern search grid and were working their way north when a crew member had spotted something. It was the hundreds of dolphins, not Jasmine, that caught his eye. And then he noticed something in the middle of the pod, a small rectangular object. At first he thought it was debris in the water. But when he saw Jasmine jumping up and down, waving her arms, he notified the pilot and marked the GPS coordinates.

The HC-130 crew circled until the chopper could refuel and come back. It was almost dusk when the Eurocopter HH-65 Dolphin returned to the scene.

Coast Guard rescue swimmer Petty Officer Third Class Ryan Stinnett was lowered out of the chopper down to the dock with a basket. As Jasmine stood up, she collapsed, but Petty Officer Stinnett caught her with one hand as he held the basket steady with the other. He cradled her in one arm and gently laid her in the basket, then gave the thumbs-up for the crew chief to raise her up to the chopper as it hovered overhead.

Aboard the helicopter and on the way to Honolulu, Jasmine realized two things. One, she would live. And two, she would marry Petty Officer Stinnett someday.

When the HH-65 Dolphin landed at Barbers Point, Oahu, an ambulance was there waiting to take Jasmine to Queen's Medical Center.

14

ARRESTED

S am and Jessica were in custody at the federal detention center on Oahu. When they were each allowed to make a phone call, Sam called his lawyer, and Jessica called Uncle Jack. She asked if he or the Coast Guard had found the cigarette boat and Jasmine. Uncle Jack said he'd located the boat in Puako, but there wasn't anyone around it. He'd found it abandoned at the dock. He'd asked around the boat ramp if anyone had seen who had gotten off the boat, and a couple of people had said it was only one guy. So Uncle Jack called the Coast Guard and told them they needed to look for Jasmine in the ocean north of VV buoy and south of Lapakahi State Park.

The DEA's Drug Task Force sent Agents Stringer and Jones from the LA office to Oahu to interview Sam and Jessica. Both agents were in their mid-forties and were seasoned investigators. Their task force had been trying to stop the flow of fentanyl to the US mainland from China via Hawaii. Since Sam and Jessica had been in possession of ten kilos of fentanyl when the Coast Guard had boarded their boat, the agents thought it reasonable to assume Sam and Jessica knew who the distributor was. The DEA didn't believe a well-connected billionaire and a former LAPD detective were the drug kingpins of Hawaii, but just the same, the feds wanted to know how it came to be Sam and Jessica were on a boat that had ten kilos of fentanyl on it.

Mr. Lau had done a perfect job of setting up Sam and Jessica. They knew they rolled the dice when they decided to go it alone without calling the FBI or Kona PD.

Agent Jones sat across from Jessica in the interview room.

Jessica had slept little the last couple of days, and the dark circles around her eyes made her look like she was a drug user.

"Ms. Kealoha, can you tell me why the boat you and Mr. Stewart were on had ten kilos of fentanyl on board?"

Jessica told Agent Jones the story of Jasmine's kidnapping and the ransom call asking for the drugs.

Agent Jones then asked, "Why didn't you call the FBI or the Kona PD?"

"The FBI headquarters is a half a dozen islands north of Kona, and I figured by the time they got here, my sister would be dead. And the Kona PD, I have trust issues with."

Agent Jones questioned Jessica for the next couple of hours and then compared notes with Agent Stringer as to what Sam had said. It was apparent they weren't the distributors that the DEA was looking for, and their stories matched. But there was still the issue of the drugs they had been in possession of. After receiving a call from their supervisor, Agents Jones and Stringer told Sam and Jessica they were free to go. But the feds were seizing Jin Tanaka's yacht, which was just fine with Jessica. Jessica didn't know who Sam's lawyer had called at the DEA headquarters in Springfield, Virginia, but it was someone near the top who had said to let them go. Just like in Hawaii, it helped to know the right people.

After being released from custody, the first thing Jessica did was check her voicemail. There was a message from a nurse at the Queen's Medical Center saying they were treating Jasmine there and she was going to be okay. Overcome with emotion, Jessica couldn't hold in all her feelings anymore. Knowing Jasmine was alive washed away the negative thoughts that she had sunk into over the past twenty-four hours. It renewed her faith that sometimes good things happened in spite of the overwhelming odds, and that it was time to be grateful and savor the moment.

After catching a taxi over to the hospital, Jessica stopped in the ladies' room so she could fix her face. She didn't mind Sam seeing her look like death warmed over, but she had this thing about always being strong for Jasmine and wanted to wash her face and put on some makeup to hide the dark circles around her eyes. Besides, she didn't want to scare her little sister by looking like a ghoul.

When Sam and Jessica entered Jasmine's room, they were surprised to find six-foot-two Petty Officer Ryan Stinnett there, standing next to Jasmine's bed and holding her hand. He and Jasmine were looking all googly-eyed at each other. Jessica went to the other side of the bed and gave Jasmine a long hug and a kiss her on the forehead.

"Are you okay, honey?" Jessica asked. Jasmine nodded, tears forming in her eyes, and they hugged again.

Ryan and Sam stood back and let the sisters have their moment together. Then Jasmine introduced Ryan. "This is Petty Officer Ryan Stinnett. He saved my life."

Sam and Jessica shook hands with Petty Officer Stinnett as he remarked with a Southern drawl, "It was a team effort. I was just one of many who helped."

Jessica instantly liked this young man. He was big as a tree and humble as a monk.

As Jessica rubbed Jasmine's hand that wasn't bandaged, she asked her, "How long are you going to be here?"

"The doctor says two days, and then I can go home."

Then Jessica pulled a photo of Woo Ching out of her

pocket and showed it to Jasmine. "Was this the guy who kidnapped you?"

Jasmine didn't recognize him from the photo because Woo Ching had disguised himself as an old man.

"Okay, honey. We have to go back to Kona and find the man who did this to you. We'll be back to pick you up when you get discharged." Jessica hugged Jasmine again, and then she and Sam left the hospital, and Jasmine and Ryan went back to making googly eyes at each other.

Sam's jet was waiting on the ramp at the Honolulu airport to take him and Jessica back to Kona. As the Gulfstream taxied toward the runway, Sam noticed Jessica deep in thought and asked, "What's bugging you?"

"I would have bet my last dollar it was Woo Ching who kidnapped Jasmine. But she says the guy looked a lot older than Woo Ching. It doesn't add up."

"What if he was wearing a disguise?" Sam asked.

"I bet you're right. I need to take this photo of Woo Ching and make him look much older and then show it to Jasmine again."

Sam frowned. "We. We need to find someone."

Jessica put her hand on Sam's thigh. "I'm sorry. I'm so used to being alone. I'll practice that *we* word."

Sam placed his hand over Jessica's. "That's better."

A few minutes later, as the jet climbed over Diamond Head, Jessica looked out the window and remarked, "I will find him, and if he resists, which I hope he does, I will kill him."

15

WOO CHING VS. JESSICA

The first thing Jessica did when she and Sam landed in Kona was to call Pua. She expected a complete ass-chewing. But to her surprise, Pua wasn't mad at her anymore. Uncle Jack had told Pua that the Coast Guard had rescued Jasmine and Jessica was in jail. The thought of Jessica locked up temporarily gave Pua a warm fuzzy feeling.

Petty Officer Stinnett had brought a cell phone to the hospital for Jasmine to use to keep in touch with her family, and him. And Jasmine had given Jessica the number when she and Sam were at the hospital. The first thing Jessica did when she got back to Kona was to use age progression software on her computer to make a series of photos showing Woo Ching from his current age of about thirty-five, all the way up to eighty years old. Then she texted those pictures to Jasmine to see if any of them looked the man who kidnapped her.

Jessica got a text back from Jasmine saying one photo looked just like the man who kidnapped her. Bingo! It was Woo Ching after all. Jessica called Uncle Jack and let him know. Now it was time to set a trap for him.

Woo Ching had been stalking Sam and Jessica since they'd

returned to Kona. He had a simple plan: slip into Jessica's bungalow and kill her and Sam. He would wait until just the right moment, when they least expected it, to strike.

Sam sent his security team back to The Racer since Jasmine was in Honolulu and safe. Jessica had decided to keep her over on Oahu, stashed away in a vacation rental until Woo Ching was in jail or dead. And Jessica didn't care which way it ended.

Jessica sensed Woo Ching was watching them. It was a feeling she had that wouldn't go away. Sam argued that his security team should hang around until they had dealt with Woo Ching. But Jessica knew if Sam's guys left Aloha Village, Woo Ching would show up and try to kill her. Especially after the intel she had gotten from Uncle Jack. He'd said Woo Ching was a notorious hit man in Hong Kong and had never failed to kill a target. Until now. His reputation was on the line. He had to eliminate Jessica, or he would never work again as a contract killer.

* * *

Jessica had made sure word got around that she and Sam were back at the Village, knowing that the mole would let Mr. Lau know. It was about nine p.m. when Sam left the bungalow and walked down to the Marlin House restaurant like he was going to get a late dinner. Jessica was wearing an innocent-looking sundress, and she walked with him out to the lanai, gave him a hug and a kiss, and watched him walk down the long driveway towards the restaurant. Then she went back inside, turned off the lights and sat on the couch and waited. Jessica had a Glock in a leg holster up under her dress to keep her company. Sam stayed away two hours, watching Jessica via a security camera feed on his phone. Nothing happened.

They repeated the same routine for another two nights. And nothing happened. No sign of Woo Ching.

The next morning, when Sam walked out the front door to

get the newspaper, a bullet ripped through his right leg as he reached over to pick up the paper. Woo Ching came running from behind a hedge of naupaka a hundred yards away and forced Sam to hobble back inside the bungalow.

Woo Ching had a silencer on the barrel of his rifle, and Jessica was in the shower, oblivious to what just happened. Comet was barking his head off, and Jessica came out of the shower to see what the commotion was about. Comet never barked unless there was a stranger at the house. She didn't want to leave the bathroom with only a towel, so she grabbed her board shorts she had hanging on the bathroom wall and a T-shirt. She opened the bathroom door and looked down the hall towards the living room.

She could see Sam sitting on the couch, holding his hand over the bullet hole in his leg, trying to stop the bleeding. Woo Ching stood in the kitchen across from him, with his rifle leaning against the wall and his pistol pointed at Sam.

Jessica could see the agony on Sam's face and the blood covering his hand. Comet sat at Sam's feet and growling towards the kitchen. Jessica knew Woo Ching was in the house. She knew he was waiting for her to walk into the living room. She also knew that as soon as she did, he would kill her and Sam.

"I know you're back there. Come on out," Woo Ching yelled.

"Why don't you come back here instead?"

"Okay, right after I kill your boyfriend."

"All right, I'm coming out," Jessica yelled. She walked out into the living room and sat next to Sam on the couch. She glared at Woo Ching for a moment, and then she said, "I'm going to give you one chance to surrender. Set the gun down on the counter next to you and put your hands behind your head, interlocking your fingers."

Woo Ching laughed as he brought his pistol to bear and then lowered the weapon as if he was considering it. Jessica had a look of contentment on her face and was glad he chose not to surrender.

Uncle Jack was in a bungalow two hundred feet from Jessica's with a sniper rifle, waiting for Woo Ching to show up and make his move. He had been in the bathroom, but when he'd heard Comet start barking, he'd run back into the living room, where he had his Remington. After checking the video feed of Jessica's house, he could see Woo Ching was going to kill them if he didn't act right that second. He aimed the rifle through the window towards the living room window of Jessica's bungalow as fast he as he could, just as they had planned. But Uncle Jack couldn't get a clear shot until Jessica sat on the couch and Woo Ching moved toward her. Woo Ching took two steps and was raising his pistol again when Uncle Jack squeezed the rifle's trigger, and Woo Ching dropped like a rock.

When the .300 Win Mag slammed into Woo Ching's chest, it must have ricocheted off a bone, and the exit wound made one hell of a mess of the kitchen.

Sam, Jessica, and Uncle Jack had rehearsed numerous scenarios if Woo Ching got in the house. Sam getting shot while going out to get the paper wasn't one of them, he reminded everyone as they waited for an ambulance to arrive.

EPILOGUE

During the investigation of Mike Murphy's crash, the FBI had questioned Simmy and noticed inconsistencies in her story right from the start. After hours of intense questioning, she'd finally admitted putting the sugar in the airplane's gas tank.

The U.S. attorney in Honolulu charged Simmy with second-degree murder but knocked it down to voluntary manslaughter, and Simmy took the deal. The judge sentenced her to five years in prison.

❀

THE SKY WAS blue and clear on the morning of Pua's first birthday party after being pronounced cancer free. Jessica had rented a pavilion at the old airport beach park for the celebration, and she and Sam had arrived early to decorate the gazebo and get ready for the party.

They placed ti leaves at each corner of the pavilion, and Sam lit the coals on the custom-built grill he'd trailered to the beach for the occasion. There was a bouncy house for the keiki, and Sam got busy barbecuing huli-huli chicken.

Over a hundred people had RSVP'd, and every starving real estate agent in town who knew Pua showed up after the food was ready.

Pua's new boyfriend, Charles, played slack key guitar as guests arrived. He was a local musician, and they had met while at chemotherapy. They were both living one day at a time and enjoying every minute together.

Jasmine and Petty Officer Ryan Stinnett arrived an hour late from Honolulu. They'd missed their flight because Ryan had been late returning from an errand that morning. He'd had to go to the Ala Moana shopping mall to pick something up for Jasmine. But Ryan wouldn't tell her what it was. He said he had to get it before they left for Kona.

Uncle Jack and Kainoa had been out on their boogie boards and were now checking the lava tide pools to see what kind of cool creatures were lurking thereabouts. Kainoa loved finding clownfish and chasing crabs. Uncle Jack had spent more time with Kainoa now that Jin Tanaka would no longer be doing so since he was in prison for possession of fentanyl.

As Pua's guests congratulated her on her victory over breast cancer with hugs and leis of different colors of plumeria flowers, a shirtless old Hawaiian man with weathered skin and long grey hair in a ponytail sat on the beach in front of the pavilion. He started rhythmically tapping his hand against an ipu drum he had carried with him. The sound of the old man's hand slapping the drum filled the air, and everyone became quiet. The combination of the heel of his hand and his fingertips hitting the drum created different sounds. It sounded like oo te oo te te over and over again.

The rhythmic beat of the drum summoned Pua, Jessica, and Jasmine as if they had been hypnotized, and they stood three abreast on the beach in front of a crowd of at least a hundred and fifty people as they performed a healing hula. They danced and connected with each other and the people in the audience. It was the healing that their family needed at that place and time. Sam had never seen Jessica dance hula before and didn't realize how much of an island girl she was until that very moment.

At the end of the hula, everyone clapped and gave the three sisters hugs. The old Hawaiian casually got up and wandered off down the beach towards town with his ipu drum.

After he'd disappeared from sight, Sam asked Jessica, "Did you know him?"

Jessica shook her head. "No." Then she looked over at Pua and Jasmine sitting nearby, and they didn't know him either.

BY FIVE P.M. all the guests had left the party, and everything was packed up. Sam and Jessica sat on the beach, waiting for the sunset. Sam hoped to see a green flash. Every time he thought he saw it, Jessica swore there was no such thing. They teased each other about it almost every time they watched a sunset together.

Uncle Jack grabbed a couple of bottles of beer out of the ice chest and came and sat down by Sam and Jessica. As he handed one of the bottles to Sam, he said he had some news.

"I thought you guys would like to know, I just got a call a few minutes ago from a friend in Honolulu that I used to work with. He said the FBI arrested Lau as soon as his plane landed in Honolulu earlier today. He was on his way back to Kona from Hong Kong when F-22's from Hickham Airforce base intercepted his plane and forced it to land on Oahu. The DEA had evidence he was responsible for a murder, and they passed it on to the FBI. So I don't think you need to worry about him causing you any more trouble."

Uncle Jack took a sip of his beer and looked towards the

ocean as two dolphins cruised by. "Go home," he yelled. He looked back at Sam and Jessica. "That was Kiki and Koa. They know the street lights are going to be on soon."

Sam and Jessica looked dumbfounded for a moment. "Only in Hawaii," Jessica muttered, shaking her head, and they all laughed.

Uncle Jack said he had fresh fish for Kiki and Koa at the *Hui Hou* and had to get back to the harbor so he could feed them. The dolphins hunted for their food during the day, but could always get a free meal if they came back to the boat at night. Uncle Jack said his good-byes and left so he could get back to the harbor before the dolphins.

Sam and Jessica watched the sun as it started to set on the horizon.

"What are you going to do now that Lau is in prison and the Village is going to be okay?" Sam asked Jessica. Before she could answer, he said, "I know what you should do. You should move in with me and Mr. Jangles at the Keauhou Bay house."

Jessica lightly rubbed Sam's leg as she contemplated her answer. She smiled and said,

"Someone does need to look after you two. It might as well be me."

"I'll take that as a yes."

Jessica scooted closer to Sam , leaning her head on his shoulder. They watched the sun disappear, and Sam saw what appeared to be a green flash.

"Did you see it?"

"Nope."

Sam sighed. "You're never going to admit it, right?"

"That's right," she teased.

The End.

I would like to give you the prequel to this book. It tells the story of the murder of Jessica's best friend when Jessica was twenty years old.

It's only available to readers of this book. Click Here to go to the download page of *Death in Hawaii*.

AUTHOR NOTES

Aloha! And mahalo for spending your time and money on this book. I hope you enjoyed it. **If you could post a review** I would be very grateful. Your review will help spread the word to other readers who might enjoy it. Mahalo!

I would like to give you the prequel to this book. It tells the story of the murder of Jessica's best friend when Jessica was twenty years old. It's only available to readers of this book.

Go to the download page of *Death in Hawaii* for the free book.

"Like" my Facebook page Hawaii Action Adventure Books to learn about giveaways, events, and more.

Want to tell me what you liked, or what I got wrong? Or what you would like to see in the next book. I'd love to hear from you. You can email me at:

Joe@JeTrentBooks.com

Or visit JETrentBooks.com/cut to read the nine chapters that didn't make it in to the final version of this book. The password is: KONA

ABOUT THE AUTHOR

J.E. Trent

J.E. Trent is an emerging author of Hawaii crime thriller novels. The Death in Hawaii Series takes place on the Kona side of the big island of Hawaii.

J.E. Trent has lived in Hawaii since 1997 and loves sharing his knowledge of the tropical paradise in his novels.

f

ACKNOWLEDGMENTS

Eliza Dee at Clio Editing. If it wasn't for her editing skill, this book would have looked like it was written by a drunk monkey.

Shane Rutherford at Dark Moon Graphics made the beautiful cover for the book.

Mahalo to all the authors who have shared their knowledge at kboards.com and the 20BooksTo50K Facebook group and many others.

HAWAIIAN GLOSSARY

Mana (Ma-Na)
Spirit
Aina (Eye-Na)
Land of the island.
Honu (Ho-Nu)
It is a green sea turtle.
Malama (Ma-La-ma)
To take care of.
Hapa (Ha-Pa)
Means mixed race. Hawaiian, Chinese, Japanese, Portuguese and Filipino make up the majority of the population in Hawaii and when they marry their children are called hapa. A mixture.

Huli-huli chicken is grilled on a trailer in a parking lot or on the side of the road. It's usually related to a fundraiser.

Da-Kine (dah-KINE) is a fill in word used for anything you can't remember the name of.

Aloha (ah-LOH-hah)
Aloha is "hello" and "goodbye." You could also have the spirit of aloha = Giving, caring.

Mahalo (mah-HA-loh)

Means "thank you."

Haole (HOW-leh)

It's used to refer to white people. It can be used offensively, but isn't always meant to be insulting. Originally it meant foreigner, but I seriously doubt anyone uses it for that anymore.

Kane (KAH-neh)

Kane refers to men or boys.

Wahine (wah-HEE-neh)

Wahine refers to women or girls.

Keiki (KAY-kee)

This word means "child." You may hear locals call their children "keiki."

Hale (HAH-leh)

Hale translates to "home" or "house." It can often refer to housing in general.

Pau (POW)

When you put the soy sauce bottle down, you may hear a local ask, "Are you pau with that?" Pau essentially means "finished" or "done."

Howzit (HOW-zit)

In Hawaii, "howzit" is a common pidgin greeting that translates to "hello" or "how are you?"

Lolo (loh-loh)

When someone calls you "lolo," they're saying you're "crazy or dumb." It's sometimes used in a teasing manner.

Ono (OH-noh)

Ono means "delicious." It can often be paired with the pidgin word "grinds," which translates to "food." So, if you eat something delicious, you might say it's ono grinds.

Ohana (oh-HAH-nah)

Means family.

BOATING GLOSSARY

Saloon = Living room. The social area of a larger boat is called the *saloon*. However, it is pronounced "salon."

Cockpit = Is a name for the location of controls of a vessel; while traditionally an open well in the deck of a boat outside any deckhouse or cabin, in modern boats they may refer to an enclosed area.

Head = Is the bathroom.

Galley = Kitchen.

Stateroom = Bedroom.

Line = Rope.

Port = Standing at the rear of a boat and looking forward, "port" refers to the entire left side of the boat.

Starboard = Standing at the rear of a boat and looking forward, "starboard" refers to the entire right side of the boat.

73084065R00092

Made in the USA
Middletown, DE
10 May 2018